RIVER OF TEETH

RIVER OF
TEETH

SARAH GAILEY

A TOM DOHERTY ASSOCIATES BOOK

NEW YORK

RIVER OF TEETH

Copyright © 2017 by Sarah Gailey

Cover illustration by Richard Anderson
Cover design by Christine Foltzer

Edited by Justin Landon

A Tor.com Book
Published by Tom Doherty Associates
175 Fifth Avenue
New York, NY 10010

www.tor.com

Tor® is a registered trademark of
Macmillan Publishing Group, LLC.

ISBN 978-0-7653-9522-1 (ebook)
ISBN 978-0-7653-9523-8 (trade paperback)

First Edition: May 2017

Foreword

In the early twentieth century, the Congress of our great nation debated a glorious plan to resolve a meat shortage in America. The idea was this: import hippos and raise them in Louisiana's bayous. The hippos would eat the ruinously invasive water hyacinth; the American people would eat the hippos; everyone would go home happy. Well, except the hippos. They'd go home eaten.

Much to *everyone's* disappointment, Congress didn't follow through on the plan, and today America lives a cursed life—a beef life, with nary a free-range hippo within the borders of our country.

Reader, this is an actual, literal thing that almost happened. The hippos are not a metaphor. You should investigate hippo ranching for yourself; as much as I'd like to call this novella the definitive text on the matter, it is most assuredly fiction. With that in mind, I caved in to my desire to make this a hippo-cowboy romp and fiddled with some dates. I shifted everything back by about fifty years, and took some liberties with what technology existed at the time in order to fit the story to the time period. I regret nothing: it was worth it for the hats alone.

For actual facts about hippo ranching, check out Jon Mooallem's fabulous piece in the *Atavist Magazine* ("American Hippopotamus").

Yours in dreams of the America that Might Have Been,
Sarah Gailey

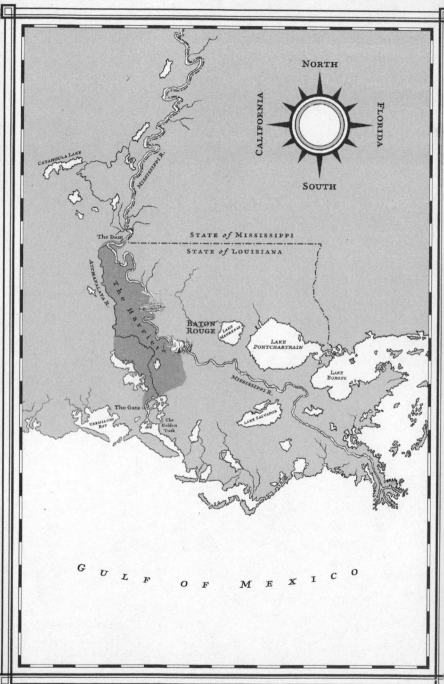

River of Teeth

Chapter 1

WINSLOW REMINGTON HOUNDSTOOTH was not a hero.

There was nothing within him that cried out for justice or fame. He did not wear a white hat—he preferred his grey one, which didn't show the bloodstains. He could have been a hero, had he been properly motivated, but there were more pressing matters at hand. There were fortunes to be snatched from the hands of fate. There were hors d'oeuvres like the fine-boned young man in front of him, ripe for the plucking. There was swift vengeance to be inflicted on those who would interfere with his ambitions. There was Ruby.

Winslow Houndstooth didn't take the job to be a hero. He took it for the money, and he took it for revenge.

The scarred wooden table in front of him was covered in the accoutrements of The Deal. The two-page contract, signed and initialed in his cramped handwriting. The receipt for disbursement of funds. A set of five photographs that had been culled from several dozen files: his team, selected after hours of arduous negotiation. There was a round-faced woman, her hair set in a crown of braids; an ink-dark, fine-boned rogue; a hatchet-nosed man with a fussy moustache; and a stone-faced woman with a tattoo coiling up her neck. The latter two were concessions he was already braced to regret. And finally—never last, only ever *finally*—there was Houndstooth himself. The photo didn't do him justice—he noted that the part in his hair was off-center by at least two centimeters—but he was wearing his finest cravat in the picture, so he'd call it a wash.

And then of course, there was the fat sack of money.

He counted out the thick gold coins, his eyes flicking to the photo of the hatchet-nosed man once every few seconds, and he waited. Now that the negotiations were over—now that his rate and his team had been established, and the money had changed hands—the small talk would begin. It was always the same with these government types. They were deeply confused by the juxtaposition of his vague accent and his eyes. His country's accent. His parent's eyes.

"So, where are you from?"

Ah, yes. There it was. They could begin the requisite dialogue about where he was from and where he was *from*. Houndstooth didn't look up from the coins.

"Blackpool." He could have made his tone frostier, but being in the presence of such a lovely stack of hard money warmed him like a milky cup of Earl Grey.

When the agent didn't immediately respond, Hounds-tooth paused in his counting, placing a mental finger next to the number "four thousand."

The agent was staring at him with such blue eyes. Such *attentive* eyes. "You don't sound British," the agent said quietly. Houndstooth found himself intrigued by the catch in the young man's voice.

"Yes, well," Winslow Houndstooth replied with a croc-odile grin. "I suppose my accent's almost gone by now. I've been in Georgia for some time. I came to the States to be a hopper, and once I tasted my first Georgia peach"—he reached across the table to touch the agent's arm, scattering the photos—"it was just too sweet for me to leave."

The federal agent's cheeks reddened, and Hounds-tooth's smile grew. He didn't move his hand.

"I do so *love* the peaches down here."

~

Winslow Houndstooth left the federal agent's office an hour and forty-seven minutes later, smoothing his hair with an elaborately carved comb. He eased the door shut behind him with a small smile.

That young man would need to take a nap for the rest of the afternoon.

The sack of gold coins was heavy, and he divided it evenly into each of Ruby's saddlebags. She could have carried the weight on one side easily—eight thousand dollars in U.S. government gold would hardly wind her—but it pleased him to know that he was flanked by four thousand dollars on each side.

He swung himself into the kneeling saddle on Ruby's back. She grunted at him.

Ruby had settled her bulk deep into the water-filled trench next to the hitching post. She wasn't made for long periods standing on land, although her breed could do it for longer than most. The Cambridge Black hippopotamus was the finest breed in the United States: sleeker, faster, and deadlier than any other hippo on the water. Ruby wasn't bred for meat; she was a hopper's hippo, meant for herding her slower, grazing cousins.

Ruby was onyx-black and lustrous; she looked like a shadowy, lithe version of a standard hippo. She stood five feet tall at the shoulder, about the height of a standard Carolina Marsh Tacky—although horses, Tackies included, were rare ever since the Marsh Expansion Project had rendered their thin legs a liability on the muddy, pocked roads. Her barrel chest swung low to the ground over short legs, perfect for propelling her through marshy waters when her rider needed to round up wayward hippos on the ranch. She grumbled on land, but could carry Houndstooth up to ten miles overland between dips in the water—another marker of her superior breeding (her cousins could only do six miles, and that only under duress). Fortunately, she was rarely out of the water that long.

"I know, girlie. I shouldn't have left you out here by yourself for so long. But you know I just can't resist blue-eyed boys." Houndstooth patted Ruby's flank and she let out a little rumble, standing under him and dripping freely for a few moments. She lifted her broad, flat nose briefly and yawned wide. Her jaw swung open by nearly 180 degrees, revealing her wickedly sharp, gold-plated tusks. They gleamed in the late-afternoon sun. She snapped her mouth shut and lowered her head until her nose nearly brushed the ground as she prepared to head home.

"Yes, alright, I know. Let's go home, Rubes, and you can keep your judgments to yourself. We need to pack up."

Houndstooth swayed with her rolling gait as she began to trot. He rubbed a loving hand over her leathery, hairless, blue-black flank, feeling the muscles shifting under the skin. Ruby was sleeker than most hippos, but not by much. Though her livestock cousins had been bred for marbling, her sub-Saharan ancestors carried little excess fat. Their rotund shape belied merciless speed and agility, and Ruby was the apex of those ancient ideals: bred for maneuverability, fearlessness, and above all, *stealth*. She was dangerous in the water: no gulls dared to plague the marshes she wallowed in, and if one was so foolish as to try to rest on her back, it would quickly be reduced to a cautionary tale for other gulls to tell their children.

"Eight thousand dollars, Ruby. We'll be able to buy our own little patch of marshland, maybe get you a bull." Ruby huffed, her nostrils—set squarely on top of her nearly rectangular snout—flaring with impatience. Her round ears didn't turn toward the sound of his voice, but they flapped irritably. Houndstooth chuckled. "Of *course* I'm joking. You're past breeding age anyway, Ruby-roo."

It was another thirty minutes to the marshside tavern where Houndstooth had a room. It would have been forty by horseback, but Ruby's trot was quicker than a horse's, even with her frequent detours to dip back into the river. Houndstooth knew when he'd picked her out that she'd grow up to be more temperamental than a slower hop would have been, but her agility had made her spirited temperament worthwhile.

She'd saved his life enough times that he figured she'd earned the right to her opinions.

When they got back to the tavern, Houndstooth un-latched the kneeling saddle and the saddlebags from Ruby's harness and set her loose in the marsh. "I'll see you in the morning, Ruby. We'll head out around dawn, alright?" She waited, already half-submerged in the water, for him to rub her snout. Her ears twitched back and forth, impatient, and she blew a bubble at him. He laughed, earning a long, slow blink of her slanting, hooded eyes. "Okay, alright, I know. You've got places to be, grass to eat." Houndstooth crouched and put a hand on either side of her broad snout.

"You're my girl, Ruby-roo," he cooed, rubbing her whiskers. "And you're the best gull-damned hippo there is."

With that, Ruby sank into the water and was gone.

~

Houndstooth propped his feet on a chair as he watched Nadine work the room. She was in her element: sliding full mugs of beer down the gleaming bar, promising to arm wrestle drunk patrons, letting customers buy her shots of whiskey to share with them (she always poured herself iced tea and pocketed the cash). He loved to see her efficiency. He'd told her many times that she would make an excellent hopper, but she always said she preferred to herd malodorous beasts that paid in cash.

She dropped off a steaming mug of Earl Grey—brewed from his own personal supply—and straightened his hat. "Where've you been, Winslow? Out with some new girl?"

He winked at her, and she tapped the brim of his hat to set it back askance.

"Ah, some new *boy*. Green eyes or brown on this one?"

"Blue," he said, toasting her. "Blue as the Gulf, and twice as hot."

He pulled out a silk handkerchief and bent to polish a scuff on his left boot. His timing was fortuitous. As he bent down, the door to the tavern burst inward and a man nearly the size of Ruby barrelled inside.

"What jack-livered apple-bearded son of a horse's ass," the man bellowed, "let a fucking *hippo* loose in a private marsh?"

Houndstooth did not remove his boots from the chair as he waved his silk handkerchief over his head. "Yoo-hoo," he said in a high falsetto, before dropping his voice down to its usual baritone. "I believe I'm the jack-livered apple-bearded son of a horse's ass you're looking for." With the hand not holding the square of paisley silk, he unbuttoned his pin-striped jacket. "What would you like to say to me about my Ruby?"

"That's your hippo?" the man said, crossing the now-silent room in a few sweeping strides. As he came closer, Houndstooth did a quick calculation. He added the bristling beard to the muscles straining at a flannel shirt and the shedding flakes of marsh grass, and he came to the obvious conclusion: marshjack. The man, it was safe to assume, spent his days scything marsh grasses to send to inland ranches. His accent was unplaceable, a combination of tight-jawed California vowels and loose Southern consonants. Houndstooth decided that he must have come South during the boom and taken up marshjacking after the bust. "That tar-skinned brass-toothed dog-eating monster out there is yours?" The man looked down at Houndstooth, who was still in his chair. "Who the hell let you on a hopper ranch, anyway? I'd like to have a word with the damn fool what thought to let you—"

"Dog-eating, did you say?"

"That's right, you yellow-bellied bastard," the man growled. "That monster of yours done *et my Petunia*."

"And what," Houndstooth inquired, easing his feet off their perch, "was your Petunia doing in that *private* marsh? Certainly not helping you hunt ducks on private property, I would hope?"

Everyone in the bar was watching them, speechless. Nadine leaned forward over the bar—the private marsh in question was her property, and so were the ducks that swam in it. The ducks she raised from eggs and sold at the market in order to pay the taxes on her bar.

"That ain't none of your business, you slick fuck," the

marshjack spat. "What's your business is that my Petunia's dead because of your painted-up hippo *bitch*."

He swung his arm. Houndstooth registered the glint of metal.

What happened next happened very quickly indeed.

Houndstooth dropped forward out of his chair and into a crouch, and the knife sailed over his head.

The marshjack's momentum carried him forward and he stumbled, his leg brushing Houndstooth's shoulder as he put out a hand to catch himself before he could hit the ground.

Houndstooth straightened, fitted his right fist neatly into his left hand, and used his full weight to drop the point of his elbow onto the back of the marshjack's skull.

There was a crack like a branch snapping. The assembled crowd in the tavern made a collective "ooh," and the marshjack fell onto his face. By the time he managed to roll over onto his back, Houndstooth was standing over him. He twirled the marshjack's long, ivory-handled knife in his hand as the marshjack's eyes eased open.

"Well, old chap," Houndstooth said in a carrying voice. "Seems you tripped and dropped your knife." He flipped the knife in the air and caught it without taking his eyes off the marshjack. "Not to worry, I've caught it for you." He tossed it again; caught it again. The marshjack's eyes followed the spinning blade.

Houndstooth crouched over him. "Now, here are some things you ought to know. One: Ruby is not painted. She's a Cambridge Black hippo, and I'd guess that's why she was able to sneak up on your dear departed Petunia. Bred for *stealth,* you see, but she can be territorial. I'm not surprised that she '*et*' Petunia, if the dog was in her waters." He tossed the knife from hand to hand as he spoke, almost lazily. "Two: Her tusks are plated in gold, not brass. It's my gold. I took it, chum, from the type of men who like to steal ducks. So you see, it *is* my business why you were in that marsh, because my Ruby-roo can always use more accessories." The marshjack tried to track the knife, but one of his pupils was dilating and he seemed to be struggling to follow the movement.

"And number three, my dear man." Houndstooth reached down and gripped the bridge of the marshjack's nose between the thumb and forefinger of his left hand. The marshjack's eyes stayed on the knife, which was now twirling baton-like between the fingers of Houndstooth's right hand. "I thought you'd want to know that they *don't* let me on hopper ranches. Not anymore." His voice dropped to an intimate murmur as the knife flashed in his hand. "But I'll be *happy* to address your concerns myself."

In one fluid motion, Houndstooth inserted the knife into the marshjack's left nostril and slit it open. Before the marshjack could so much as choke on his own blood, his right nostril had been similarly vented.

Winslow Houndstooth straightened and wiped the blade of the knife clean on his handkerchief. He dropped the square of ruined silk onto the marshjack's face just as the man raised his hands to clutch at his filleted nose.

"I'll help you clean up the sawdust tonight, Nadine. Sorry about the mess." Houndstooth stepped over the marshjack and shot his cuffs, raising his voice over the marshjack's moans. "Oh, and I'll be paying out my room this evening. I've got a business trip to go on and I think I'll be a while."

Nadine set two glasses on the bar and poured a measure of whiskey into each as the bar patrons slowly began to converse again.

"Where ya headed, Winslow?"

He took a photo out of his breast pocket. The hatchet-nosed man glared up from it, his wispy moustache abristle. "The Mississippi River, sweet Nadine." He tossed the marshjack's fine ivory-handled knife in the air; it flipped end-over-end five and a half times before dropping, point-down, through the hatchet-nosed man's left eye. Houndstooth clinked his glass against Nadines. They each downed their whiskey, and Houndstooth gave Nadine a wink and a grin to go with the burn in both their throats. "And what a fine river it is."

Chapter 2

NOBODY EVER SUSPECTS THE FAT LADY.

Regina Archambault walked through the market with her parasol over her shoulder, plucking ripe coin purses from pockets like fragrant plums from the orchard. Her hat was canted at a saucy angle over her crown of braids. Many of her marks recognized her, the visitor they'd sat next to at church or at a fete. They greeted her by name—and then their gazes slid off her like condensation down the side of a glass.

And she helped herself to whatever she deemed that they didn't have a use for. Rings, watches, wallets, purses—the peacock feather from the back of a particularly lovely bonnet. They never seemed to suspect that a woman whose dresses were custom-made to fit over her broad body would have nimble fingers. That she would be able to slip past them without drawing attention.

"Archie! Oh, Archie, you dropped your handkerchief!" A young gentleman in a beautifully felted bowler hat ran after her with a flutter of pink clutched in his outstretched hand.

"Now, Aaron," she said, archly but in low enough tones that they would not be overheard. "You know full well that is not my 'andkerchief. I did see one just like it for sale in the general store, though." Aaron flushed, and he smoothed his downy moustache with a nervous forefinger. Archie stepped with him into the entrance of an alleyway, where they could be away from prying eyes.

"Well, Archie—that is, Miss Archambault—that is—I just supposed that I might—"

Archie reached out her hand and took the handkerchief. "Aaron, mon amour—you know we mustn't let anyone see us together like this. Why, think how they'd *talk*." Her fingers rested on his for a moment as she took the little scrap of pink from him.

He leaned toward her. "Archie, I have to talk to you about our *plan*. I think my parents suspect something, and I won't be able to get away tonight after all."

His father, the stern patriarch of the wealthiest family in New Orleans, certainly did suspect something—he suspected quite a bit, if he'd read the anonymous letter Archie had sent him. She pressed the pink handkerchief to her lips and summoned tears to her eyes—just enough to brim prettily. "Oh, mon ciel étoilé, but I must go first thing tomorrow! And you must come with me, and we *must* buy the tickets this evening! I suppose—you'll just have to give the money for the train tickets to me and I'll buy them, and I'll—I'll 'ide one in the knot in our tree for you to collect when you can join me. You *will* join me, won't you, mon amour? You . . . you remember the tree I'm talking about?" She dabbed delicately at her eyes with the handkerchief and fluttered her lashes at him.

"Oh, yes, Archie, I—I remember. How could I forget where we—" If he had been any pinker he'd have been a petunia. He pulled an envelope from his vest pocket and pressed it into her hands, looking over both of his shoulders as he did so. "Here's the money for the train, and . . . I'll see you at the station, then?"

Archie pressed the handkerchief to her eyes again, so he wouldn't see her roll them at his ham-fisted attempt at stealth. "A kiss, Aaron. For luck." She kissed him hard—a better kiss than the boy would likely ever get again in his life. She kissed him thoroughly enough that he wouldn't notice her fingers dancing through his pockets.

"I'll see you at the train station in two days, my love."

She waved her handkerchief at him as he crept out of the alley, and she tucked the fat envelope of cash into her reticule. The poor little overripe peach of a boy—she marvelled at the way he walked, with the confidence of someone who's never been hungry or cold or heartbroken before in his life. When he was out of sight, she examined his pocket watch. A fine piece—it would fetch a fine price. Just *fine*.

She straightened her wide-brimmed straw hat and left the alley, gathering her skirts around her. She turned down a side street, away from the crowd, and walked to a broad old dirt road. A dog ran between two of the pecan trees ahead of her. Other than him, she was alone, and she walked down the middle of the road, parasol dangling from her wrist, holding her skirts up with one fist and her hat down with the other.

As she walked through the pecan trees to the marsh dock, the hidden pockets in her overskirt thumped against her leg.

As she scanned the water for Rosa's white ears, Archie whistled—a tune she'd heard from a busker in the marketplace. She couldn't remember the words—something about a hopper and a debutante—but the melody was catchy.

A stream of bubbles moved across the surface of the water. *Aha.*

"Rooo-saaa," Archie sang in her lilting alto. "I seeee-youuu!"

A white blur erupted halfway out of the water and rushed the dock. Archie swept her hat off, spread her arms and set her legs in a wide stance as the three-thousand-pound albino hippo splashed toward her at full speed.

"Bonjour, ma belle fille!" Archie cried. "Mon petit

oeuf douce, 'ave you been having fun while maman was at the market?"

Rosa skidded to a stop a few inches in front of the dock. Archie tapped a long finger against the hippo's broad white nose.

"You, ma cherie, need to get sneakier. You're too easy to spot!"

Rosa shoved her snout against Archie's drooping skirts. "Yes, fine, 'ere—" Archie unclasped her skirts and pulled them off, revealing close-fitting red pinstriped riding breeches underneath. "—I got you a pastry, cherie. I know that cruel veterinarian says you shouldn't, but we don't 'ave to tell 'im about this, do we?"

Archie pulled a slightly squashed turnover from the pocket of her skirt and held it out to Rosa's nose. The hippo's pink eyes remained unfocused, but she turned unhesitatingly toward the smell of the tart. Her mouth swung open, and Archie dropped the turnover onto her tongue.

"Aren't you scared she'll bite you?"

Archie whipped around, startling the sallow, bone-thin boy behind her so much he nearly fell off the dock. She grabbed his arm and hauled him away from the edge of the planks.

"Of course I'm not scared," she said, still gripping the boy's arm. "I've 'ad Rosa since she was just a petit 'op.

She would no sooner bite me than she would join the Paris Opera. Sneaky little urchins who follow me, on the other 'and—" She smiled and brought her face close to the boy's face, close enough that she could have bitten the brim of his cap. "She eats them up without a thought."

The boy swallowed hard but was not foolish enough to wriggle out of her grip. "Please, ma'am, you *are* Miss Regina Archambault, aren't you? They told me to look for the, uh, the—"

"The fat Frenchwoman with the albino 'ippopotamus?" Archie deadpanned.

"Uh, yes, miss. I—I have a letter for you. Please don't feed me to your hippo, ma'am, I didn't mean to sneak—"

He raised a trembling hand with an envelope in it. Her name was written on the outside in familiar, spiky lettering. Archie released his arm.

"Well, then, that is something else altogether." She grabbed the letter. "Would you like to pet a 'ippo, boy?" He looked nervously at Rosa's tusks. "She will not eat you. Not unless I tell 'er to. Just make a lot of noise as you walk up, so you don't startle 'er—'er eyes, they are not so good."

The boy glanced between Archie and the pink-eyed hippo. "I've never heard of a blind white hippo before."

"Well," Archie said, "the 'opper that bred 'er was going to kill 'er when 'e saw. 'What use is a blind 'ippo?' 'e said. But I knew better—she is the finest 'ippo in all the world."

The boy stared at Rosa, awe plain on his face. "Her name's Rosa?"

Archie ran her thumb under the seal on the envelope. "Oui. Let 'er smell your 'and, then you can scratch behind 'er ears."

As the boy approached the beast, tentatively placing a small hand against her snout, Archie read through the letter.

"Well, well," she whispered to herself. "Winslow, you old connard," she said, not looking up from the letter. She murmured to herself as she read it through again. "Ferals . . . eight *thousand* . . . a full year? Non, that can't be—oh, oui, I see now . . ." She turned to the boy, who was staring at Rosa's tusks with rapt fascination as he rubbed her nose. She looked him over, taking in his dull, patchy hair and his anemic complexion. She wondered if he slept in the streets, or if he hadn't escaped the orphanage yet.

"Miss Archa-Archim—"

"Call me Archie."

"Miss Archie? You said you had her since she was just a hop, right?"

"Oui," Archie replied. The boy was looking up at her with shining eyes, one hand resting on Rosa's nose.

Archie lowered her voice conspiratorially, just to watch his face light up. "Hoppers, you see, we apprentice for years—then we choose a hop, when the time comes. We sleep beside them, we feed them, we sing to them. We're with them every moment of their lives, from the time the cord is cut to the moment they're fitted with a harness."

The boy's eyes were wide. "So that's why you're not scared of her?"

Archie laughed so heartily that the boy began to look sheepish. "I'm sorry, boy, it's just—I couldn't imagine being less frightened of sweet Rosa." Rosa, hearing her name, yawned wide, showing off her teeth. The boy stared into Rosa's massive mouth, his face aglow with awe.

"How do you get her teeth so white?"

Archie smiled. "I brush them. Would you like to see?"

The boy nodded, reaching out a now-fearless finger to touch one of Rosa's gleaming tusks.

"I'll show you, if you run a little errand for me. I need a telegram sent to a Mr. Winslow Houndstooth. Can you remember that?" She told him the message she wanted sent to Houndstooth, and she gave him a coin to get her a map of the Mississippi River.

"Be back here in two hours, and I will show you 'ow I brush her teeth. Hell, I'll even let you 'elp me pack up 'er saddlebags."

The boy put a hand on top of his cap, as though afraid it would fly off in the wake of his excitement. "Oh, boy, Miss Archie, I'll be back faster'n you can spit!"

He ran down the dock, his feet flying up behind him. Archie smiled, and turned back to Rosa, who was waiting patiently to see if another turnover would be forthcoming.

"Well, cherie," Archie said, folding her laden skirts over her arm. "It would appear that Winslow is calling in our old debt. I suppose I could argue that I owe 'im nothing after what 'appened in Atlanta—but what's a favor between friends, oui? 'E's got a job for us, my Rosa. How would you like to be a rich 'ippo?"

Rosa grunted, lowering herself further into the marsh. Archie pushed her skirts into a half-full saddlebag, then slipped off her shoes and sat on the dock, dangling her feet in the water. She rubbed a wet foot over Rosa's half-submerged nose. "Eight thousand dollars. Just think, Rosa. Think of the pastries I'll buy for you."

Chapter 3

HERO SHACKLEBY DID NOT READ the letter when it arrived.

They didn't read the second letter either.

They read the third, but only because it was hand-delivered.

Hero sat in their rocking chair, watching the tar-black hippo with the gold-plated tusks amble up the road. It would stop in front of their house, to be sure. Hero didn't look up from the sweet tea they were stirring as the hippo came to a stop at the bottom of the front steps.

"You can pop her in the pond with Abigail. Gate's around the side there."

The man on top of the hippo didn't respond, but dismounted and walked around the side of the house. Hero listened as Abigail greeted her new pondmate, as the man in the peacock-blue cravat cooed to—ah, yes. "Ruby," he called her. Abigail was a Standard Grey—not too far off from a meat hippo, but considerably smarter. She would be friendly to Ruby. She was friendly to everyone. *Hospitable,* Hero thought.

Hero stirred the iced tea, tasted it. *Not quite there yet.*

Ruby's rider came back around to the bottom of the front steps. He put his boot on the first step, then stopped, his chin tilted toward Hero's face. "Might I join you?"

"S'why I've got a second rocking chair," Hero said, assessing the man out of the corner of their eye. He was tall, immaculately dressed. He had cheekbones that sliced right through the thick, golden afternoon sunlight. He walked up the steps deliberately, watching Hero. Watching Hero's pistols.

"Don't worry," Hero said. "I won't shoot you. Sweet tea?"

"You haven't been reading my letters," the man said.

"You're English. Lancaster?"

"Blackpool. You haven't been reading my letters."

"And you haven't accepted my hospitality," Hero said, gesturing to the unoccupied rocking chair and the sweet tea sweating on the porch rail in front of it. "Please, won't you sit?"

The man sat. He looked like he wanted to sit on the edge of the rocking chair, but it was canted so that he had to sit all the way back. He held his hat in his hands. "My name is Winslow Houndstooth. I got your name from the federal agent who gave me this." He dug into his pocket and held out a thick gold coin with an eagle on it. "He said you'd want this job."

Hero sipped at their sweet tea, ignoring the proffered coin. "Hot this summer. They said it would be cooler, but I'd say it's a sight hotter than it was this time last year."

Houndstooth tapped the coin against the arm of his rocking chair. "I wouldn't know. I've never been to this part of Louisiana before. Rode here all the way from New Orleans. And that after the steamship ride along the Gulf."

"Your Ruby must be tired as a hog after a boil."

"She seemed happy to get into the water. Your Abigail looked damn bored in that pond, though. I bet she'd like the work." He pulled an envelope from his jacket pocket and handed it to Hero.

"I'm retired." They considered Houndstooth over the rim of their glass. "But I'm glad you came to tell me about this 'job' in person. Like a gentleman."

Houndstooth's eyes found Hero's. "Shackleby. That's an honest name. Are you an honest person?"

Hero smiled, close-lipped. "I'm not a liar. Ask me anything and I'll tell you the truth."

"Is that sweet tea poisoned?"

Hero's smile broke into a broad grin. "I thought you'd never ask." They picked up the second glass of sweet tea from the porch rail, took a sip, and set it back down. "See? I'm just fine."

Houndstooth didn't touch the glass.

"Abigail is bored," Hero said after a moment. "She's not used to living in one place, to having her own pond all to herself. She loves it. Has her own little dentist-bird." Hero leaned their head back against the rocking chair and fanned themself with the letter. "But she's bored. I haven't saddled her up in months. It's just been the two of us, all alone, plus the milkman once a week. And I don't even drink milk."

"Hero." He seemed to be rolling their name across his tongue. Hero caught themself staring and looked away. "Hero, I'm supposed to get you to accept this job. I accepted this job with the understanding that I would have a demolitions expert on board."

Hero sipped their sweet tea and watched Houndstooth fiddle with his hat. "I'll need some convincing. So. Convince me." They tried not to blink while they said it, knowing that it sounded for all the world like a line. Houndstooth's eyes snapped up, and he swallowed hard. Hero rubbed a tapered forefinger through the condensation on the outside of the pitcher of sweet tea.

"Well," Houndstooth said in a low voice. "There's the money. Eight thousand dollars. Gold, not bonds."

"Hmm." Hero ran their finger down the side of their throat, letting the cool water cut through the heat of the afternoon.

"Then there's the job itself," Houndstooth said. "Clearing the feral hippos out of the Mississippi. You'd live up to your name, if we managed it. We'd be heroes, Hero."

"Mmmhm." Hero leaned back in the rocking chair and crossed their legs, right over left. It would be something, to be a *hero*. A decent way to end a career that had gone on too long. Better than simply fading off the scene, like they'd planned. They tapped their nails on the arm of the rocking chair, one-two-three-four.

"And then, of course, there's the team. It would be you and me—" He paused for a moment. "—Archie the Con, Cal Hotchkiss, and Adelia Reyes."

Hero sat forward at this last name. "Adelia Reyes? I thought I heard she was—"

"Yes," Houndstooth interrupted. "But she'll still do the job. She never turns down a job."

"Well." Hero sat back, folding their hands in their lap. "It sounds like you've got quite a team already. Without me. So why would you need me, Winslow Houndstooth? Why do you want to pull me out of the retirement I've been so thoroughly enjoying?"

Houndstooth stood and turned on his heel, leaning his back against the porch rail. His hand rested next to the untouched sweet tea, which had begun foaming softly. He looked down at Hero, his gaze unwavering.

"Because," he murmured. "I think you want it."

Hero was thankful that their skin was dark enough to conceal the hot flush that was climbing their neck.

"I think you've only been retired for a year, and already, you'd poison a stranger just to break up the monotony." Houndstooth knocked the sweet tea off the porch rail. It hissed as it ate through a rosebush. He leaned forward, still holding the porch rail. "I think you'd enjoy working this job a lot more thoroughly than you've enjoyed sitting in that rocking chair."

Hero looked at Houndstooth's burning eyes. "Is that what you think?" they asked, and sipped their sweet tea to relieve their suddenly dry mouth.

"Yes. That's what I think. That," he said, tilting his head to one side, "and I've got some things I need blown up. From what I hear, you're the one to do it."

Hero set their glass down and stood, clapping their hands decisively. "Well, then." They walked inside, and emerged a few moments later wearing a battered leather Stetson and clutching a large, bulging duffel.

Houndstooth laughed. "I thought it would take more convincing than that!"

Hero walked toward Houndstooth until their boots touched. The laughter on Houndstooth's lips died. They were nearly the same height, and their noses were less than an inch apart. Hero could smell the sweet iced tea on their own breath.

"Ask. I know you're wondering. If we're going to work together, you may as well ask."

Houndstooth swallowed. "I . . ." He paused, looking down at Hero's mouth, then looked back at their eyes. "How did you drink the poison? Without it killing you."

Hero blinked. That wasn't the question they had anticipated. "I'm immune. Small doses. Every day."

Houndstooth smiled. "Well. That's the only question I need the answer to." He sat back down and unfurled a map of the Harriet on the table between them. "Shall we plan a route? I think we should be able to get into the marshes by midmorning, and then we can collect Cal before meeting up with the rest of the crew. . . ."

Hero let themself smile as they sat across from Houndstooth and began studying the map. This *would* be more fun than retirement.

Chapter 4

HOUNDSTOOTH WATCHED OUT OF the corner of his eye as Hero stretched their arms high over their head. The popping of their spine as they twisted made Ruby startle; her tail flapped irritably in the water of the marsh.

Hero and Houndstooth had been riding since dawn. The day's ride had been filled with long, easy silences and the slow, steady rhythm of Ruby and Abigail's treads through the water. The shadows were growing long as the sun began to dip, and Houndstooth had just started to doze off when Ruby's flicking tail splashed water down the back of his shirt.

"Ah! Damn." He wiped his brow with his handkerchief, then reached back into his saddlebag. The day was hot; the air was thick enough that even the mosquitoes seemed to be flying a little slower. Houndstooth swatted at one that was trying to find its dinner on the back of his neck; then he reached back into his saddlebag, pulled out two pears, and tossed one to Hero, who caught it without looking.

"Show-off," he said with a small smile.

"Sleepyhead," Hero drawled back.

Houndstooth was about to object, but interrupted himself with a huge yawn. He tried to cover it by biting into his pear, but Hero was already laughing at him.

"Keep me awake, then," he said through a mouthful of pear. Hero raised their eyebrows and Houndstooth felt himself blushing. Hero let it lie for a moment before answering.

"Alright, if it's my job to keep you stimulated. Let's talk about your grand . . . caper."

"It's not a *caper*, Hero. It's an operation. All above-board. All very well-planned and prepared-for."

"And what's the plan?" Hero asked.

Houndstooth coughed. "I was hoping you'd help me come up with that."

Hero bit into their pear, spat a seed. "You're funny." They said it without smiling. They tossed the top third of their pear into the water in front of Abigail, who snapped it up without missing a beat. Abigail crunched and swallowed the pear, twitching her ears.

"That I am," Houndstooth said cheerfully. "Have you ever been to the Harriet before?"

"No," Hero said, "I'm not one for gambling."

Houndstooth looked at them sidelong. He dipped his hand into his saddlebag and scooped out a little pouch of the white saddle-resin all hoppers used to keep their kneeling saddles from sliding around on the slippery, hairless backs of their hippos. He dipped his finger into it and drew a long oval with open, fluting ends on Ruby's inky shoulder, where Hero could see it. He drew a thick line across the top third of the oval, where the narrowed end flared open again—the dam that had turned the Mississippi into the Harriet. Not quite a lake and not quite a marsh, the Harriet was a triumph of engineering, but the ferals trapped within it rendered it a national embarrassment. The riverboat casinos that dominated its surface did little to alleviate the distaste with which most of the country considered the entire region.

"So, if this is the Harriet, then this is the Gate." Houndstooth drew another line across the bottom third of the oval. Hero snorted.

"You're not much of an artist, are you?"

Houndstooth glowered at them. "This is the Gate," he continued. "It keeps the ferals inside of the Harriet, so they can't get out into the Gulf. The Gate at the bottom of the Harriet and the dam at the top keep the ferals penned." He smudged white on each side of the circle. "Unbroken land to the east and west for a few miles in all directions keeps the ferals from traveling to other waters."

"So, it's . . . what? Twenty miles overland in every direction?"

"Give or take," Houndstooth said with a shrug. "It's enough land that the ferals can't make it across. I'm sure a few try every year, and die in the process. Either way, the Gate extends far enough inland to discourage them from making a serious attempt at migration."

"Do they want to leave?"

Houndstooth chewed on this. "I doubt it," he said after a minute. "They've been there for a few breeding generations. It's all they know. And other than the riverboats, it belongs to them."

Hero nodded. "Alright. So this plan that you're expecting me to come up with is supposed to motivate these dangerous, well-entrenched animals to migrate *south*."

Houndstooth grinned at them. "That's right. Per the federal agent who hired us, all we have to do is get them through the Gate," he said, drawing a line from the middle of the oval out through the bottom line on the crude map. "And then they're in the Gulf, and they're not our problem anymore." He drew the white line of resin all the way down Ruby's flank and into the water, making Hero laugh. Their laugh was infectious, and Houndstooth found himself laughing too as he splashed marsh water onto Ruby's back, rinsing the map away.

"What does the Coast Guard think of this plan?"

Houndstooth shrugged. "They're not the ones paying me."

"And what do the riverboat casinos think of it?"

"That's a good question," Houndstooth said. He settled his hat low over his eyes, and the two sank into the easy silence of the humid afternoon.

There would be plenty of time for Hero to learn about the Harriett, Houndstooth thought. Plenty of time for them to learn about the man who had shaken enough hands and bought enough half-destroyed land to practically own the surface of that feral-ridden puddle.

Travers.

If he had a first name, nobody seemed to know it. If he had a soul, Houndstooth had certainly never glimpsed it. Travers had seen an opportunity when the Great Hippo Bust of '59 rendered half the marshland in Louisiana worthless. He'd made his first fortune purchasing parcels of land for pennies apiece and reselling them to the Bureau of Land Management for use in developing the Harriet. The only caveat had been that he would have unfettered, exclusive business rights on the water, and the right to deny access to any nongovernmental person seeking entry via the Gate.

It was a story that most hoppers didn't know, but then most hoppers hadn't done business with Travers. Unless they'd spent time on his riverboats, most hoppers didn't know how much he relied on the vicious, hungry ferals that infested the Harriet. There had been a time when he would have paid handsomely to have even hungrier beasts in those waters.

There had been a time.

Hero interrupted Houndstooth's blood-soaked memories of the most dangerous man in Louisiana. "So, we're getting the ferals out of the Harriet because—why?"

"Trade route," Houndstooth murmured without looking up. "The dam is crumbling already—there's a huge crack down the middle, and it's less stable every year. The plan as I understand it is to tear it down and reopen the Harriet to trade boats that need to get down to the Gulf. But the boats won't go through if there are ferals eating their deckhands. So, they've got to go."

"Ah, right. That's not what I meant," Hero said. "I meant why are *we* doing it? What's in this for you?"

Houndstooth missed the comfortable silence. He swayed back and forth on Ruby's back, listened to the lapping of marsh water against her barrel chest. Abigail nudged Ruby with her shoulder. Ruby grumbled and ducked her nose under the water, and Houndstooth felt the pressure of Hero's patience settle over him.

"Have you ever had anything that you feel like you'd die without?" Houndstooth said it so quietly that it sounded like a prayer. "Something that you've put everything into—your whole life, all your heart? Have you ever had anything like that?"

There was another long minute of silence as Hero thought it over. Ruby blew bubbles in the water with her nose. On the shore of the marsh, a trio of fat frogs hopped into the water. Abigail glared at the shore primly, affronted by the commotion.

"I don't think I have," Hero said. They sounded distant, but when Houndstooth looked over, they were patting Abigail's flank with a small smile.

"I had a ranch once." Houndstooth watched Hero out of the corner of his eye, from under the shadow of his hat. He was ready for them to be skeptical, ready to have to prove his credentials. Hero didn't look back at him; they simply braced their hands on the pommel of Abigail's saddle and tilted their head back, their eyes half-closed. Houndstooth managed not to stare at the bead of sweat that ran down the side of Hero's long throat. "A breeding ranch."

"Takes time, saving up for a ranch," Hero drawled without opening their eyes.

"Fifteen years," Houndstooth replied. He found himself watching the water to keep from watching Hero. Ruby left barely a ripple in her wake; the mosquitoes that landed on the water didn't move out of her path. "It took fifteen years of work to buy the land. I started when I was seven years old, bottle-feeding sick hops at my uncle's ranch outside Atlanta every other summer. My father wouldn't pay for my passage across the ocean, so I worked throughout the year to get the money—I did whatever I could, short of stealing." He swallowed back memories of his father's reaction the one time he'd attempted to pick a pocket. "One year, I just didn't go back home. I stayed, so I could work the ranch year-round."

"That's when you knew," Hero said. It wasn't a question.

"That's when I knew," Houndstooth answered. He took his hat off and used it to scoop up a patch of mostly clean water, dumping it over Ruby's back to keep her skin from drying out. "I was the best breeder in the country, you know. Back before my ranch burned. Could have been the best in the world."

Hero didn't ask what had happened. They rode in silence for another thirty minutes or so as the sun dipped low, kissing the tree line. They set up camp a few miles outside the Harriet Gate. There would be no fire that night, but the air was warm enough that they didn't need it. They laid out their bedrolls and sat, listening to the cacophony of nighttime insects and frogs singing. They passed a flask of whiskey back and forth while Ruby and Abigail splashed and grumbled in the water, looking for good patches of grass to dine on. The sky went grey; a few bright stars announced themselves. There was no moon, but the star-filled sky cast just enough light for Hero and

Houndstooth to see each other's outlines.

After a few more minutes, Houndstooth grunted, leaning back on his bedroll and propping himself up on his saddlebag. "I'm going to kill the man who burned down my ranch, Hero. You should know that."

Hero stared hard at him. "If that's what you have to do to make something right," they said. "If you feel ready for it."

"I've been getting ready for years, Hero," Houndstooth murmured. "He's been hiding from me on the Harriet. And I've been waiting for the need to kill him—the hunger for it—to die down. But it hasn't. And now?" He patted his saddlebag. "Now I have a warrant to get onto the Harriet, and not even Travers can turn me away at the Gate."

By way of an answer, Hero held out the flask. Houndstooth reached up for it. He misjudged the distance in the dark, and his fingers closed over Hero's wrist. They both froze for a moment—then, Houndstooth slid his hand up over Hero's. His fingers felt their way slowly past their hand, past their fingers, over their fingertips, finding the flask.

Houndstooth unscrewed the top of the flask, taking a long drink. Then, finally: "I wish you could have seen it. The ranch."

Hero's murmur only just carried over the hum of insects that rose around them. "Tell me."

It was the kind of story that couldn't have been shared by daylight. Houndstooth told Hero about the ranch—about the hard year he spent preparing the land he'd bought near the Harriet, about the harder year he spent getting his hands on good breeding stock. As the darkness thickened and solidified, he told Hero about sleepless nights spent nursing newborn hops back from the brink of death. He told them about hiring his first ranch hand, Cal—the man they were on their way to collect. He tried to show them a scar he'd gotten from his very first breeding bull—a thick rope of shining skin that cut across the inside of his bicep and ran almost all the way to his collarbone. He unbuttoned his shirt to show Hero where it met his shoulder.

"I can't see it," Hero laughed. "It's darker than the inside of Ruby's belly out here, Houndstooth."

Houndstooth set down the nearly empty flask and grabbed Hero's hand. "Here," he said, and before he could think he had pressed their fingertips to the scar. His breath caught.

"Are my hands cold?" Hero whispered.

"No," Houndstooth murmured back, as Hero's fingers traced the full length of the scar where it met his shoulder. He could smell the sweet whiskey on their breath.

"What happened?" Hero asked, their fingertips still

on Houndstooth's collarbone.

"Well, the bull was trying to kill a nine-month-old hop, and I—"

"No," Hero interrupted Houndstooth. "What happened to the ranch?"

For the space of three of their shared breaths, the only sound was the buzz of night insects and the flap of Ruby's ears in the water. Then, just as Hero was preparing to draw a breath to apologize for asking a question they knew they shouldn't have, Houndstooth answered.

"He burned it down." His voice broke on the word "down," as though he couldn't quite hold the notion that the ranch was really *gone*. He lifted his hand and impulsively placed it over Hero's.

"I woke up one night, middle of the night. I'd been in . . . in the birthing barn." He cleared his throat but didn't stop telling the story. His fingers tightened briefly over Hero's. "I'd been in there all night, working through a difficult labor. It hadn't looked good—I almost lost the mother three or four times. My hands were white and wrinkled from being underwater so long, trying to shift the hop into the right position to come out. But then, like nothing had ever been wrong at all, that mother just up and pushed out her hop. It was small, but it swam right up and poked its head out of the water and took its first breath, no problem. It was a healthy, perfect little girl-

hop. The cow was looking at me like she didn't know why I thought I needed to interfere." He let out a breath that was almost like a laugh. "I was so exhausted, I fell asleep right there on the marsh grass beside her.

"When I woke up, the barn was filling with smoke. It smelled . . . wrong. I'll never forget it, Hero." He was nearly whispering, and Hero leaned a little closer to hear him. His voice was thick with the memory. "I stumbled outside and tripped over the hop, the one that had just been delivered. The mother was nowhere in sight—but then, I could hardly see anything, the smoke was so thick. There was sweat in my eyes, it was so hot, and the fire . . . the fire was *everywhere*.

"I picked up the hop and ran. She was small, small enough for me to carry, and too new to wriggle like they do. I got to the edge of my marsh and set her down in the water—her skin was already getting dry—and then turned to run back and put the fire out, but—" He stopped midsentence, and Hero could hear him trying to find the words.

"It was too late," they murmured.

Houndstooth sniffed hard. He squeezed Hero's hand once, hard, and then let it go. He leaned back on his bedroll, resting his head against his saddlebag again. After a few minutes, he went on.

"I couldn't go back through the fire. The marsh grass

was just dry enough, and there was a wall of flames be-tween me and the paddocks. I couldn't see through the fire and the smoke, but I could hear them," he said. "The air smelled like . . . like *meat*, Hero. It was all wrong. I could hear them thrashing, bellowing. I could hear the hops. I could hear them burning. A hundred in all, hops and mothers and bulls, and I stood there and listened to them die." His voice broke, and there were another few minutes in which they both pretended his tears were silent ones.

"I stayed there, as close as I could be without choking on the smoke, and I watched it burn. All the hippos I'd spent my life breeding—gone. Dead." He fell silent.

"What about the hop?" Hero asked after a moment.

"Ah, well, of course," Houndstooth answered, his voice still thick. "She started nudging at my ankles around dawn, as the flames died down. She was hungry enough that she started trying to suckle on the toe of my boot. She raised up well enough, didn't she?"

"She sure did," Hero answered. "Jesus, Winslow. A hundred hippos." They whistled long and low. "That must've been a helluva ranch you built."

"It was," he replied. "It really was." He laughed mirth-lessly. "But after it burned? I had nothing left but bad debt. I had to sell the parcel to Travers to get out from un-der it." Houndstooth spat into the water. "And look at me now. What do I have to my name? A bedroll and a grey hat and Ruby. The last of her line. And her getting older every day."

Hero put their hand near the edge of their bedroll. Their pinky finger brushed against Houndstooth's. He didn't pull his hand away.

"A few weeks from now, that won't be all you'll have," Hero murmured.

"No?" Houndstooth said, linking his pinky finger with Hero's.

"No," they replied. "In a few weeks, you'll also have revenge."

Chapter 5

"THEY DON'T HAVE HOPPERS in California, asshole. They don't have *hippos* in California."

"Well, Alberto," Cal Hotchkiss said to the balding off-duty ranger, shifting his toothpick from one side of his mouth to the other, "that's your opinion."

The four men around the table were not looking at each other. They watched the cards in their hands as though nude women were painted on the fronts of the cards, instead of the backs. They were not wreathed in smoke—the riverboat casinos did not allow smoking in private suites—but three of them chewed on unlit cigars. Cal Hotchkiss preferred his toothpick.

"It's not an opinion," the tall black man in the black hat chimed in. "There's no hippos in California. No rivers. No marshes. Means no hippos."

The men accepted cards from the dealer, who kept his eyes downcast as he slid them across the felted top of the table. They slid the cards into their hands, muttering to each other about the Sacramento River and whether it featured marshes; none of them knew, and Cal declined to educate them. Alberto sniffed. He leaned toward the window, holding onto his grey felt hat, and spat a thick stream of tobacco into the water. A moment later, a soft splash sounded.

"You know what they do have in California?" The man in the black hat took a sip from the mint julep that rested on the felt in front of him. "Adelia Reyes."

For a moment, none of the men seemed to breathe. The only sound was the creaking of the giant wheel that propelled the riverboat slowly forward.

The moment passed.

"Never heard of her," Alberto said. "Edvard, you heard of her?"

The fourth man at the table—a squat Swede in a bolo tie—shook his head. "If I had heard of her, I sure as shit wouldn't want to hear of her again."

Cal Hotchkiss didn't say anything at all. He laid out his cards. The rest of the men at the table seemed to exhale as one as they each acknowledged defeat. Cal reached out one long arm and hooked it around the pile of chips in the center of the felt, reeling in his winnings. He lifted his bowler with one hand and ran his fingers through his damp, white-blond hair. The breeze coming in from the open window just behind his chair ruffled the fine wisps of his moustache. "Well, gentlemen. I win again." He lifted his hat high in the air, and a dark, doe-eyed waitress wearing a breathtakingly low-cut corset slid over. She leaned close to him, her perfume wafting around the table.

"Yes, Mr. Hotchkiss?"

"I'd like a drink, Cordelia. And then I'd like for you to come and sit in my lap."

"Right away, Mr. Hotchkiss."

She walked out of the small room to fetch a drink from the main floor of the casino, and the other men at the table watched her go—all of them except for the man in the black hat.

"Going to take her to bed with you, Cal?"

"Nah." Cal shrugged, slipping his winnings into the pockets of his jacket. He looked sharply at the man in the black hat. "Mr. Travers wouldn't like it."

The man in the black hat smiled. "Of course. It's nice to meet you, Cal Hotchkiss. Name's Gran Carter, U.S. marshal." He flipped up his jacket to reveal the silver star that hung from his belt buckle.

"I know who you are."

"Then maybe you know why I'm here."

"Maybe I don't give a shit."

The pit boss walked past the doorway and the dealer made eye contact with him. A moment later, the dealer had melted away from the table, leaving the four men alone with the dregs of their drinks. Alberto turned to

Gran Carter. He was more than a little drunk. "Look here, Mister Marshal, I ain't done nothin' wrong here no how, an' I've got a badge too, see, I'm a *ranger* for the Bureau of Lan' Management, an' I fancy I've got even more pull here than the likes of—"

Gran Carter clapped Alberto on the back hard enough that he choked midsentence. "You're alright by me, friend. I'm not here for you, and I'm not here for the casino, and I'm not here to stop Mr. Travers from throwing cheats into the river. Hell, I'm not even here to make Mr. Hotchkiss shave that embarrassment of a moustache." He reached into the breast pocket of his jacket. All of the men around the table reacted instantly, drawing pistols and pointing them at the U.S. marshal in the broad black hat.

"Woah there," he said, holding up his hands. In one of them, he held a photograph. The men around the table put their guns away—all except Cal, who merely lowered his to the table. He kept one hand on the gun. The other hand reached up unconsciously to stroke his patchy blond moustache. At that moment, Cordelia arrived with a tray and handed a glass of honey-brown liquor to Cal. She perched in his lap like a cat sitting on a fence post, her eyes fixed upon his unholstered revolver.

Carter set the photograph on the table and slid it toward the center of the felt. "That there's Miss Adelia

Reyes, gentlemen. I happen to know that she was on the Harriet eight or nine months ago, and I'm guessing she talked to some people here. She owes me a conversation. I'd be much obliged if y'all'd look over that photograph and tell me if you've seen her."

None of the men took the photograph, but their eyes all locked onto it the same way they'd been watching their cards before the game had ended. The sepia photograph showed a woman with burnished bronze skin and the cool, steady gaze of a contract killer. She stared out of the photo with hawkish, predatory eyes; a tattoo of a thorny vine coiled its way up the side of her neck and into her hair.

"Well," said Edvard. "I think I'd remember it if I ever saw a lady like that. What'd she do that a marshal's looking for her?"

Alberto rubbed a thick rope of scar tissue on the back of his left arm. "I'd imagine she killed a man."

Carter looked at Alberto with that unwavering smile. "You'd imagine right."

Cordelia leaned over the table to look at the picture, then opened her mouth as if to speak. Cal Hotchkiss rested his hand on her hip, his grip tight. She closed her mouth without speaking.

"Well," Carter said, pushing back from the table and standing without taking the photograph. "I'll be around if you need me."

Edvard and Alberto stood together and walked over to the bar, shooting glances at Carter as he sauntered toward the exit. Cal watched him walk away, then stood. Cordelia toppled from his lap. He grabbed a wad of cash from the center of the table and thrust it at her. "For the drink. And the company. Go on and tell 'em downstairs that I'll be along shortly to pick up my Betsy."

"No need," a cheerful voice rang out from just behind them. "I've already moved her into a paddock for some quality time with my Ruby."

Cal whipped around so quickly his hat fell off, leaving Cordelia to gather the bills he'd dropped. In the instant it had taken him to turn, he'd grabbed his revolver off the table and unholstered a second, smaller gun from his belt. He had both pointed at Winslow Houndstooth with the hammers cocked back by the time his hat hit the ground.

"Now, Calhoun, that's no way to greet an old partner." Houndstooth strode toward Cal, plucking his bourbon from the table and sampling the bouquet deeply before taking a long, slow sip. Behind him, Cordelia slipped out of the room. "Oh. That's very fine, indeed. You still have excellent taste."

"You here for me, Houndstooth?" Cal growled. "If you think I'll go quiet, think again." He shifted his toothpick back and forth in his mouth.

Houndstooth laughed. "Nothing like that, Cal, my old friend! I'm here to work with you again. Partners. Just like old times. Just like back on the ranch." Houndstooth flicked open a long, thin stiletto blade and twirled it between his fingers like a baton. "You remember the ranch, don't you, Cal? The one you worked on, right up until it burned to the ground on the same night you ran off to work on the Harriet? A fine coincidence, that."

Cal started to edge toward the door. Houndstooth stepped swiftly between him and the exit. "Love the—is it a moustache you're working on? We really must catch up, Calhoun, old chap. I've been wanting to have a *chat* with you for some time now."

A cough sounded from the door. They both turned, and the air in the room went cold. Hovering in the doorway was a sleek little stoat of a man, his pencil moustache slicked across the top of his lip like a drunk draped across a chaise longue. His seersucker suit was fitted to him so impeccably that Houndstooth's breath caught for a moment in his throat.

"Gentlemen. I trust you're both familiar with the rules of my casinos." The man's voice was smoother than the bourbon his bartender poured for high rollers.

"Mr. Travers," Houndstooth said. "I wasn't going to hurt my old friend Cal, here. Just showing him my new knife."

"And a fine knife it is," Travers responded, inclining his head. "It would be such a shame if it were to get wet. And your pistols, Mr. Hotchkiss—I don't imagine they stand up well to submersion?"

Cal and Houndstooth stared at each other for a long moment. The boat creaked as they watched each other. Travers cleared his throat, and they both lowered their weapons.

"Very good. Now, I'm sure you gentlemen would like to have a civilized discussion over drinks at the bar? On the house." He waved an arm toward the door. The two men hesitated, neither wanting to walk in front of the other—but after a beat, Houndstooth put his grey hat on, tipping it to Travers.

"I'll be waiting for you with a whiskey, Calhoun, old friend. We've got business to discuss."

He walked out without a backwards glance. Cal made to follow, but Travers put out a hand before Cal got to the door. Cal stopped before Travers so much as touched him.

"Now, what precisely do you suppose he's doing here?" Travers murmured, his voice as silky as a snake's belly sliding over a bed of marsh grass.

"I got no damn idea," Cal growled. Travers considered him for a long, silent minute. "I said I don't *know*," Cal said, his eyes flicking away from Travers'. "And whatever it is you're thinking you'll ask me to do about it, I ain't doin.'"

In just three unhurried steps, Travers crossed the room and was behind the chair near the window, where Cal had been sitting. He stooped, looking like a heron that had spotted a fish. When he straightened, he was holding three playing cards. He held them up where Cal could see them. Cal's face didn't so much as twitch. Travers dropped the cards onto the felt of the table and spread them out with the manicured tip of his index finger.

"Three Queens. Were these insurance against losing, or did they come in handy at some point while you were fleecing my customers?"

Cal shook his head as his lips went white. Travers held up a quelling finger.

"Shhh, no, don't try to lie to me, Mr. Hotchkiss. You were cheating. You were *stealing* from me. Oh, yes, I know, you weren't stealing my *money*, Mr. Hotchkiss—but you've tarnished my name. You've put my reputation into question, and you've made me look foolish." His voice hadn't risen above a murmur, but it dripped with menace. He whipped the silk pocket square from his jacket and, turning to the open window, laid it across the broad sill. "You realize that this is your second warning?"

Cal nodded.

"And you realize, don't you, that there will not be a third warning?"

Cal nodded again.

"Let's just be sure, why don't we? It always pays to be thorough. Come here."

Cal shook his head again, unable to form words. His face had turned a peculiar shade of grey. Travers gestured with one elegant hand, then unbuttoned his cuffs and began to roll up his sleeves.

"Come now, Mr. Hotchkiss. *Cal.* Let's not waste time. Your friend is waiting, after all." He finished rolling up his sleeves, then checked to make sure they were of equal lengths. That done, he snapped his fingers. Cordelia entered, holding a domed silver tray. She did not look at Cal as she passed by. She set the tray on the gaming table near where Travers stood, where he could reach it without moving away from the window.

"Thank you, Cordelia, darling." Travers smiled at her with warm eyes. She smiled back, tentative. He nodded to the door, still smiling, and she left, ignoring Cal's desperate attempt to catch her eye on her way out. After she'd disappeared from sight, two massive men stepped in from the hall—Travers' security. They turned away from the room, so their backs filled the doorway. Cal let out a strangled sound like an aborted whimper.

"Mr. Hotchkiss," Travers said. "I don't have all day. Do not make me ask you again."

Cal crossed the room with slow steps. Sweat beaded on his brow as he watched the covered tray. The only sounds in the little gaming room were his shaky breathing, the creak of the steamboat wheel, and the lapping of the Harriet.

Travers uncovered the little silver tray. There, on top of a folded maroon napkin, lay a gleaming, curved hunting knife—Cal's hunting knife, taken from his room on the boat. It had been cleaned and honed since he had seen it last. The edge of the blade was so fine that his eyes couldn't quite rest on it.

Travers picked up the cards from the felt-topped table and laid them down in a neat row on the square of silk he'd laid across the windowsill. He rested the tip of one manicured index finger on the center card.

"Are these your Queens, Mr. Hotchkiss?"

Cal swallowed hard, a muscle twitching in his jaw. He nodded. Before he had finished nodding, Travers' hand flashed out, and Cal's face slammed into the windowsill. His right cheek was pressed against the three Queens. Travers' hand was smashed flat against the left side of his face, holding him against the sill. The corner of the top card pressed against the right corner of Cal's lower lip, sharp. The tips of Travers' fingers dug into the flesh of

Cal's face, his grip as firm as bone.

Travers slowly bent his head until his eyes were level with Cal's. The heel of his hand ground painfully against Cal's jaw.

Travers picked up the knife.

"Are these your Queens, Mr. Hotchkiss?"

Cal made another strangled sound. Sweat dripped into his eyes. He finally managed to open his mouth wide enough to rasp the word "Yes."

Travers brought the knife to rest just under Cal's left eye, then traced it along the top of his cheekbone, just lightly enough to leave the barest red scratch. Cal felt a single tear work its way out of his right eye. It fell through the open air, all the way down to the water.

"Look," Travers hissed. And Cal did.

He looked down, following the path his tear had taken. He couldn't move his head, but he strained his eyes. His breathing hitched as his gaze found what Travers wanted him to see: the ferals.

The water swarmed with them. They stayed near the *Sturgess Queen* during daylight hours, while the sun warmed the water around the riverboat to a temperature they could abide. They circled it hungrily, waiting for someone to cheat or brawl or get handsy with one of Travers' girls. Waiting for Travers' security staff to hurl someone overboard, so they could fall, flailing and screaming, into the water.

Cold sweat ran down the small of Cal's back as he watched the ferals look up at the boat, impatient for their next meal.

Travers let him sweat for a full minute before he asked the question a final time. "Are. These. Your. Queens."

Cal choked out the words. "Yes, Mr. Travers, sir."

There was a flash of movement. Cal's left ear felt suddenly hot, searing hot, and then there was pain, blue-white and filling the left side of his head. He spasmed, but Travers' hand gripped his face, and he could not lift his head from the windowsill. He could not lift it even as blood filled his ear, muffling all other sounds in the room—even as it poured down the front of his face, stinging his eyes. He tried to draw breath to scream in pain but ended up sputtering, choking on a mouthful of his own blood.

Travers held him there with a firm hand, taking slow, deep breaths. He held the knife out in front of him, over Cal's head. Balanced on the edge of it was the lower half of Cal's left ear.

Eventually, Cal stopped thrashing and was still. His breathing was labored and ragged; blood covered his face, stained his collar, pooled around his cheek. It would have run down the windowsill, but for the square of silk that just barely managed to contain the puddle of blood.

Travers lowered the knife so Cal could see his ear, as delicate as a magnolia petal.

"I don't give third chances, Mr. Hotchkiss," Travers murmured. He licked a fleck of saliva from the corner of his mouth with the pink tip of his tongue. He twitched the knife. The severed half-ear landed directly in front of Cal's eyes.

Travers finally released Cal, but the blond man didn't stand up right away. Travers grabbed the purple napkin from the silver tray, and used it to wipe his hands clean before dropping it on Cal's head.

"You should get cleaned up," he murmured, staring at the bleeding man with flat, passionless eyes. "I expect Mr. Houndstooth will be waiting for you. Oh, and Calhoun?" He waited for Cal to straighten and look at him before continuing. "Not a *word* to Houndstooth." He pulled a linen handkerchief from his back pocket with a flourish. He used it to pick up the piece of Cal's ear that still lay on the windowsill; then, he wrapped the ear up with quick, delicate motions, and dropped it into his breast pocket.

Cal's eyes were locked on the pocket that had half of his ear in it. "Yes, Mr. Travers, sir."

"Very good." Travers turned and left the room without another word. Cal stared after him, clutching the purple napkin to what was left of his ear. After a minute or two, he swore under his breath. He left the room, still pressing the napkin to the side of his face. Houndstooth was waiting for him.

Chapter 6

THE HARRIET INN was the only bar in the slim mile between the Gate and the Gulf with its own pond. All the hoppers that came through town stopped there sooner or later to enjoy the excellent service and the brutal atmosphere. The darts were sharp and the drinks were strong. Cal and Houndstooth arrived together, and, without speaking to each other, they spread themselves out at a low, scarred table. They ordered the first round, and several mugs of beer arrived well before anyone else did.

Houndstooth lit a long, slim, black cigar, and blew a stream of smoke at Cal, who chewed his toothpick as though it had wronged him.

"So," Houndstooth said. "You quit?"

"I got all the smoke I needed ten years ago." Cal smiled around his toothpick. The smile did not extend beyond the corners of his lips.

Houndstooth ashed his cigar directly onto the tabletop. He stayed at the Harriet Inn as frequently as any other hopper, but he felt no affection for the place. It was only ten years old, and it still smelled to him of smoke and burning hops. It rested on the grave of his old ranch: Travers had used the land to build the Harriet Inn, so that anyone too drunk to get home from the Harriet had a place to lose the remainder of their money.

"You know," Cal said in a conversational tone, "if I didn't need the money to pay off Travers, I'd just as soon kill you."

Houndstooth took a pull on his cigar and let the smoke curl out of his nose. "Really?" he asked. "Because I could just as easily *not* find Adelia for you. I'm sure she'd rather not be found. Especially not by a man she went *fugitive* to avoid."

Cal bit his toothpick in half. He did not respond.

Twenty minutes of thick, heavy silence later, toward the butt end of Houndstooth's cigar, Archie walked in. She sat on the bench with her back against the wall, avoiding the too-small chairs that surrounded the other three sides of the table.

"Well, hot damn. If it isn't the great Regina Archambault," Cal drawled, putting unnecessary emphasis on "great" as he fingered the bandage that covered his left ear.

"Call me Archie," she said, not looking at him. "Winslow, do you 'ave another one of those cigars to share? I've been on the road all goddamned day."

As Houndstooth pulled his cigar case out of his pocket

and cut a fresh one, the door eased open. Hero slid in, melting easily into the shadows of the dimly lit bar, and slipped into a chair.

"Well, that's it. We're all here."

"Un moment, s'il vous plaît," Archie said. She whistled a few short, high notes, like birdsong. A towheaded boy poked his head into the bar. She signaled him, and he perched on the bench next to her.

"This is Neville. 'E is my assistant."

The table was still for a moment; then, everyone looked at Houndstooth. Archie addressed him directly, ignoring Cal and Hero.

"I trust 'im, Winslow. The boy knows where 'is loyalties lie. Plus, 'e knows that if 'e ever betrays us, I'll gut 'im like a one-legged 'op. Isn't that right, Neville?"

Neville nodded strenuously, looking only at Houndstooth.

"Well, if you trust him, Archie, then I suppose he can stay."

Archie ashed her cigar onto the floor, satisfied.

"Well," Houndstooth said. "Let's all get to know each other. You all know me, so I'm not going to introduce myself—forgive me, Neville, you'll just have to figure me out on your own time." Neville nodded again, with vigor.

"Archie," Houndstooth said, gesturing with the stump of his cigar, "is the finest con either side of the Mississippi. Her meteor hammer can take down a charging bull faster than anyone I've ever seen. She's saved my life nine and a half times."

"Ten," Archie said, grinning around her cigar.

"Nine and a half," Houndstooth responded with a smile. "Also, she's got a connection to a certain U.S. marshal of whom we don't want to run afoul." Cal looked as though he had a comment to add. Archie levelled a pitiless stare at him, and he thought better of it.

"Hello, Archie," Hero said, extending their hand. "I've heard so much about you."

Archie shook Hero's hand. "Charmant," she said, and to the surprise of everyone at the table, it sounded for all the world like she actually meant it.

"From what I've been told," Houndstooth continued, "Hero there could blow up a bank vault using a pile of hippo dung and a cup of water, and they could make it look like an accident. Plus, they could poison a hummingbird and it would dip its beak twice before it dropped. They're smarter than I am, which is saying something. And they're—" He coughed, took a sip of his drink. "They're, ah, they're just a great team member."

"What kind of a name is 'Hero'?" Cal muttered around his mangled toothpick.

"It's my name," Hero responded.

Cal spat splinters into the sawdust on the floor, then

selected a fresh toothpick to maim. Archie raised her eyebrows. "And who is this charming young man?"

"Calhoun Hotchkiss," Houndstooth said archly. "He's the fastest gun in the West."

"I'm the fastest gun anywhere." Cal responded with the speed of deep-seated bitterness over the title.

"He's also the only one of us that's ever dealt with ferals," Houndstooth added. "Aside from Adelia Reyes, if we can find her. He's spent years working on the Harriet. He knows everything there is to know about it. He's stupider than he looks, but he shouldn't hold us back too much."

"And what about you?" Cal retorted. "What do you bring to the table, you smug fuck? Who made you the boss?"

Houndstooth was evidently ready for this question. His hand flicked, and before Calhoun could flinch, there was a tiny click on the table in front of him. All the eyes at the table fell on the sliver of wood that suddenly lay in the puddle of condensation left by Cal's beer.

Cal reached up and felt for his toothpick, which had been sliced cleanly in half.

Houndstooth rested both his hands on the tabletop. One of them held the same stiletto blade he'd drawn on the riverboat.

"I'm the boss, Calhoun Hotchkiss, because I'm faster than you. I'm smarter than you. I'm *better* than you. And

I'm the one who can send the telegram that will get you paid at the end of this. So here's what's going to happen: you're going to get us into the places that only your reputation can get us into. You're going to shoot fast and you're going to shoot straight. You're going to be helpful and respectful. If you don't do those things, then you don't get paid. Is that clear?"

Cal drew a fresh toothpick from his pocket and inserted it into his mouth, saying nothing.

"Good," Houndstooth responded. He glanced around the bar. It was empty but for them and the bartender. "Now, we need to find the fifth member of our crew." He slid a photograph into the center of the table—the same photograph that Gran Carter had left sitting on the felt of the poker table earlier that day. Adelia Reyes stared unsmiling out of the photograph. Everyone at the table examined the photograph, but it was Cal who reached for it first. He looked at it for a long time, swallowing hard; then he set it back in the center of the table and stared at his hands for a few minutes, clearing his throat every few seconds.

"You're all familiar with Adelia Reyes. She's been missing for seven months."

Cal coughed. "Seven and a half."

"Right," Houndstooth said, frowning at Cal. "Seven and a half months. She rides two hippos: a Standard Grey

73

and an Arnesian Brown. She switches between the two so she doesn't have to rest either one—so we'll probably find her near the water somewhere. Can't travel overland with two hippos for long."

Neville, who had been silent until that point, raised his hand. Archie gave him a quelling look, but he kept his eyes fixed on Houndstooth, who, after a long minute, waved a hand at the boy.

"Sorry to interrupt, Mr. Houndstooth sir, but I've seen that woman."

All eyes at the table swivelled toward Neville.

"You've what?" Hero and Archie said at the same time. Cal looked at the boy with an intensity so sharp it put Winslow's knives to shame.

"I've seen her. Just now, outside. She was . . . well, she was at the tobacconist, sir. She looked . . . a little different from how she looked in that photo, sir. She spotted me 'n Archie, and while I was putting Rosa up in the pond out back, she came by the water to visit, and she—" He met Cal's eyes and paused.

"She what, Neville?" Hero asked gently.

"Um, well." Neville turned to Houndstooth. "She came by the pond, and she took a look at Ruby—that's the hippo with the gold tusks, right? She looked inside Ruby's mouth and asked if I knew who rode her here, and I said I didn't, and then she looked at the other grey in the pond, the one with the nasty scars? She talked to that one for a while."

Cal sucked in a breath at this and looked back down at his hands. A little blood had started to soak through the bandage over his ear.

Houndstooth sprang up from the table and made for the door. Archie gave Neville a little shove. "Go after 'im, now. Show 'im where you saw 'er."

But before Neville could get up—before Houndstooth made it across the bar—the door burst open. A woman walked in and stood, silhouetted in the doorframe until the door swung closed behind her.

She took a few steps forward, into the light, and took in the crew assembled around the scarred old table.

"Well," Adelia Reyes said. "Well, well, well." The most brutal contract killer of the late nineteenth century folded her hands over her distended belly and winked at Calhoun Hotchkiss, before settling her gaze on Houndstooth. "I'd be willing to bet you're looking for me, Mr. Houndstooth."

The crew assembled at the table watched as the outline of a tiny foot pressed at Adelia's shirt. She pressed a hand to it. "Shhh, mija. Mama's working."

Calhoun slid sideways off his chair and fell to the sawdust on the floor, unconscious.

"Hello, Adelia," Houndstooth said. "How would you

like to make eight thousand dollars?"

Adelia pulled out a chair, not minding too closely whether the chair's legs smacked into Cal's head. She sat with her legs spread wide to accommodate her belly, resting a foot on Cal's neck. She smiled at Houndstooth, her hands stroking the shifting mass of her stomach.

"Well," she said softly, "what's the job?"

Chapter 7

IT WAS QUIET IN THE SWAMP. Deep quiet—the kind that's defined by the buzz of insects and the lapping of water and the thick wet heat of the day. The shade of the willow and sycamore trees that grew along the edge of the water dappled the golden light, but their shade wasn't enough to cut through the weight of the heat. The hoppers rode slowly, easily—they shared an unspoken need to enjoy the calm of the swamp. It would be their last peaceful day. Soon, they'd reach the Mississippi Gate, and the chaos would begin.

Adelia rode Stasia, her heavily armored Arnesian Brown, without a saddle. She rode cross-legged, one hand wrapped around her belly; the other gripped the pommel of Stasia's harness. Stasia, an exemplar of her breed, snapped at birds that flew too close to her snout. She grumbled at sticks that bumped into her legs, and squinted suspiciously at the other hippos. And yet, for all her aggression, she seemed devoted to Adelia—Adelia, who swayed with Stasia's rolling gait, occasionally singing nonsense to her in lilting tones. "Stasia, my Anastasia, Ana Aña, Aña-araña . . ."

Neville rode next to her on her second hippo, Zahra. He knelt awkwardly in the borrowed saddle, but Zahra—an aging Standard Grey, nearly identical to Abigail save for the livid bolt of white across her brow—followed Stasia gamely, ignoring the way the boy pitched to and fro in the saddle.

"Miss Adelia, this is so *hard*," he said, out of breath from struggling to maintain his balance. "How come you can do it without even a saddle?"

"I have been doing it since I was in my mother's belly," she replied with a wisp of a smile. "When my little niña is born, she will ride with me, and she will be just as strong as I am. Stronger, perhaps."

"What if it's a boy?" Neville asked, clutching at the saddle.

"It won't be a boy."

Neville stared at her for a few moments without speaking, his eyes lingering on her belly.

"You are wondering about the father," she said, un-smiling. Neville stammered an incoherent denial, his blush destroying his credibility.

"There is no father," Adelia said. "There is a man who gave me the child I wanted from him."

Neville stared hard at his hands. "Alright ma'am," he whispered, mortified. She grinned at his embarrassment.

"I am not ashamed, boy. I have no need of a husband. This girl will have no need of a father. Perhaps a second mother, someday—but if not?" She shrugged. "It makes no difference."

A sharp whistle sounded from behind them, where Archie rode her diamond-white Rosa. Neville twisted in the saddle to look at her, then caught himself on the pommel as he nearly tipped out of the saddle. Adelia whistled back without looking away from the water ahead. Archie's rich, deep laugh carried over the sound of the hippos' splashing progress through the shallows of the swamp.

Ahead of them, Cal, Houndstooth, and Hero rode abreast. Ruby slid through the water like a shadow between runty brown Betsy and Hero's grey Abigail. Shy, sweet Betsy bumped out of the way with a sidelong glance at the sleek black hippo, but Abigail didn't seem to notice her. Ruby came close enough to Abigail that Houndstooth's leg brushed against Hero's. Hero startled.

"I didn't—I didn't hear her get so close," they said, holding their hat on with one hand.

"Well, you wouldn't, would you?" Houndstooth said. "Some things just sneak up on you like that."

Hero tried to stop the smile that spread across their face, but it was too late; Houndstooth was already grinning back.

~

As dusk settled over the marsh, the hoppers clustered closer together. Houndstooth rode in front. Behind him, Adelia, Archie, and Neville clustered together. Hero and Cal rode behind, occasionally shooting wary glances at each other.

"So, I've been wondering," Adelia said. "What is that for?" She pointed at the coiled chain that Archie wore on her hip. "It looks like the strangest bola I've ever seen. I can't imagine using it to disable a man, much less a charging hippo."

Archie smiled. "I adore your idea of small talk, Adelia. This is my meteor 'ammer." She patted the smooth metal ball that swung beside her thigh. "I will show you 'ow it is used sometime. I think you will like it."

"It's really somethin', she showed me on the way here," Neville piped. "She swings the chain around her whole entire body and then she just turns and whips it and *pow!*" He slapped Zahra's flank. The hippo didn't seem to notice. "It just *crunches* whatever she aims it at!"

"I hope I don't have a need to see it in action," Adelia said, "but I would love to see a demonstration." She looked at the meteor hammer and for a moment, genuine affection ghosted her features. "At any rate, we should find a place to tie up," Adelia said. "It's unwise for us to be in the water after sundown."

"Oui," Archie said. "And we should go over the plan for this caper before we turn in."

"Why?" Neville asked.

"It's not a *caper,*" Houndstooth replied, sounding irritated. "It's an *operation*. All aboveboard."

"Well, we still need to go over the plan," Adelia snapped.

"If you see a dry patch I don't," Houndstooth said, slapping at a mosquito, "you go right ahead and point it out."

"There was a petit island a mile back or so," Archie mused, "but too small, I think, for all of us."

"Why can't we be out after dark?" Neville asked again.

"Too small for your fat ass, maybe," Cal called from the back of the group. Archie's fingertips played over the revolver that hung from her hip.

"He's not worth the bullet," Adelia murmured to her.

"Why shouldn't we be out after dark?" Neville piped.

"I could stab 'im, perhaps," Archie said, giving Adelia a wry smile.

"Si, but then the blood would ruin your lovely blouse."

"Excuse me," Neville said again.

"Strangulation, then. The cleanest death of them all," Archie continued, ignoring him.

"Ask Hero for some poison, maybe?" Adelia and

Archie both laughed. Hero smiled from under the brim of their hat. Neville looked back at Hero, eyes wide.

"You have a lot to learn, boy," Hero drawled. "Never stare at someone you're scared of."

Archie smiled over at Neville. "Are you scared of Hero?"

Houndstooth chuckled. "I'd imagine he's scared of all of us."

Hero fanned themself with their hat. "Oh, son. You shouldn't be scared of us. Us, you'll see comin'. No, what you want to be scared of," they said, looking at the boy with a wicked gleam in their eye, "is the *ferals*."

Neville clung to Zahra's back. "I ain't scared of hippos." His voice shook a little.

"Well, young man, there's hippos and there's hippos," Cal said. "Now, Zahra there, she's a sweet thing. Raised by people from when she was just a little hop. Slept next to her hopper's raft every night, ate from her hopper's hand every day. Loyal. Loving. But a feral?" He laughed mirthlessly.

"Let's not scare the boy," Houndstooth said. "He won't be seeing any ferals anyway. They're all between the Gate and the dam, and he won't be going in there with us."

"You never know," Cal intoned.

"Is . . . is that why we have to find a place to camp before nightfall? Because of ferals?" Neville asked.

"That, and Cal is scared of the dark," Archie said loudly. "So let's 'urry it up, oui?" She snapped her fingers twice and Rosa surged ahead, nudging her white nose against Ruby's coal-black flank.

They found an island just as the sun dipped below the horizon. The hum of insects intensified as the last light of the day died, and the hoppers guided their steeds toward the little hump of land that rose out of the water. Archie whistled to Neville. "Would you care to give Rosa's teeth a brush before we turn 'er loose for the night?"

Neville grinned, his sweat-damp blond hair falling into his eyes, and he held up a leather pouch. "I've already got her toothbrush, Miss Archie!" He splashed down the riverbank, cooing to Rosa. The white hippo had already begun to wander away from the sandy bank of the islet. She had been riding all day, and was reluctant to come back to the shore before she'd eaten. The sound of Neville's coaxing entreaties for her to come back for a brushing drifted through the stillness of the dusk, blending with the buzz of cicadas.

"'E is a good kid," Archie said ruefully, settling onto a log beside Hero.

"He's too green to be out here," Hero responded. They pulled out a pocketknife and began scraping the bark off a fat stick.

"Ah, 'e'll be fine. I couldn't leave 'im behind," Archie

said. "Rosa, she likes 'im too much for me to tell 'im no, when 'e asked to come. Just like Houndstooth. I could never say no to 'im, either."

The sounds of Houndstooth and Cal arguing over where to start the fire drifted to them through the warm night air.

"You really care about Houndstooth, eh?" Hero asked.

"I could ask you the same question, couldn't I?" Archie responded with a grin. Hero looked up, not returning Archie's smile.

"You know, when I first met Houndstooth, 'e had just had 'is 'eart broken. 'Is dream—it was in ashes. I watched 'im meet someone, a woman. I watched 'im fall in love with 'er."

Hero's brow furrowed, but they did not interrupt.

Archie waved her hand vaguely. "She ran off with a postman. They were going to go north, to the cities. Tried to take Ruby with them, but of course Ruby, she would not go. She is devoted."

Hero considered Archie. "So . . . what happened after that?"

"Ah," Archie said. "Houndstooth started to sow 'is wild oats. As for the girl? Well, I will not say. Houndstooth . . . 'e does not need to know what I did to the girl when I found 'er trying to steal Ruby. But I will tell you this"—Archie looked at Hero, her face serious—"what I did to 'er will look like a kindness, compared to what I will do to anyone who breaks 'is 'eart like that again."

Hero stared into Archie's eyes, unblinking. "I understand."

Archie clapped them on the shoulder, hard, smiling warmly. "I know you do. I can tell. I just 'ad to say it—you know 'ow it is. Ah, don't be too scared. I think you are good for 'im! You should see 'ow 'e smiles at you when 'e thinks you are not looking. Plus, you keep 'im from thinking 'e is the smartest in the room."

Hero smiled, ducking their head; then, they looked up, the smile suddenly gone. "Did you hear that?"

"What," Archie said, "are they finally just comparing their cocks and 'aving done with it?"

But Hero was already on their feet, running to the water's edge.

They were too late.

By the time Hero had reached the riverbank, Neville was half-submerged in the water. There came a fierce splash, and the boy surged into the air before landing, caught, in the gaping mouth of the feral bull.

He hung in the mouth of the beast, stunned. His left leg hung between the bull's front tusks, the angle wrong. It bled freely, and his blood spilled over the hippo's whiskers. Archie covered her mouth with both hands when she caught up with Hero as though to catch the boy's name even as she shouted it. Cal and Houndstooth looked up and came running. The bull was still for a long, thick moment. Then, with a lightning-quick twist of its thick neck, it snapped its jaws closed.

The boy was dead. There could be no question, even before the feral bull shook him below the water. Archie turned away; Hero put an arm around her, shielding her as much as possible from the bloodied swamp water that sprayed the shore. Cal and Houndstooth stood frozen a few yards from the water's edge, empty-handed. Cal's toothpick dangled from his slack lower lip.

They did not see Adelia coming.

Neither did the hippo.

It wasn't until the beast was bleeding that Houndstooth registered her standing next to him, her arm outstretched toward the hippo as though she was offering it a handshake. Houndstooth looked from her to the bull, which twitched and writhed spasmodically in the frothy pink water.

He put a hand to his pocket, as though he'd find anything there; but of course, it was empty. The long, slender, ivory-handled knife he'd taken from the marshjack back in Georgia was gone. A mere inch of the handle still protruded from the bull's eye socket. The rest of the knife was buried in the beast's brain. A trickle of blood spilled over the hippo's cheek like tears as it gave a final thrash, and then sank below the surface of the water.

As the ripples stilled, Adelia lowered her throwing arm.

"That," Cal said quietly, "is why you shouldn't be in the water after sundown."

Chapter 8

DRAGGING THE HIPPO'S CARCASS out of the lake wasn't easy, but it had to be done: Rosa, Ruby, Betsy, and Abigail wouldn't approach the shore with the bull's blood pinking the muddy water. Zahra and Stasia were nowhere to be found, but Adelia seemed certain that they'd return at dawn so long as the bull's carcass was gone.

Fortunately, none of the hoppers was a stranger to dead hippos. Archie insisted that she be the one to wade out into the swamp—insisted that it was her fault the boy had been in the water in the first place. She secured a length of rope around her middle and made her way to the hippo while Cal and Houndstooth watched the water, ready to haul her back in if so much as a bubble surfaced nearby. She girded the beast with five separate ropes before splashing back to the shore. They all hauled him onto the sand together, dragging him far enough inland that their hippos wouldn't be disturbed by the smell of their mad, dead cousin. Had they been on a ranch, they'd have butchered the carcass and sold the hide to a tannery; as it was, nobody could bring themselves to take a knife to the creature that had so efficiently slaughtered young Neville.

The exhausted hoppers dried themselves around the fire, not acknowledging the fact that none of them would volunteer to wade back into the river to find Neville's body. Cal was the first to break the silence.

"I think it's time you told us the plan, Winslow. You *do* have a plan?"

Archie looked at him, hollow-eyed. "Yes, 'oundstooth, what is the plan?"

Hero was the one who answered. They reached into their bedroll and pulled out a map of the Harriet, spreading it on the ground a safe distance from the fire and weighing down the corners with empty, whiskey-sticky mugs. The map showed the lake, enclosed parenthetically by the dam to the north and the Gate to the south. The feral's usual territory, near the center of the lake, was marked with a large red circle; the safe travel routes, by blue arrows. The rest of the marks on the map were incomprehensible at first glance.

"Dynamite," Hero said, pointing to a concentric series of red X marks on the map. "Here, here, and here—all around the northern perimeter, just far enough from the dam to be safe. A series of controlled explosions that will drive the ferals toward the Gate." They pointed to the next row of X marks below that. "Then another series, here, and another here, just south of that one. The idea is to keep the detonations behind the ferals, driving them closer to the Gate, not giving them a chance to double back."

"Like a funnel. A hippo funnel," Houndstooth added.

Archie examined the map, nodding. "And we will have the Gate open, right? So they just scoot out into the swamp and then head down to the Gulf?"

"Exactly," Hero said. "We close the Gate behind 'em, spend a few weeks rounding up any stragglers—and then sit back and enjoy the Harriet for the rest of the year."

"And how does the Coast Guard feel about this?" Archie asked.

"Don't worry about it," Houndstooth said peevishly. "The Coast Guard isn't where the money's coming from, so they're not our problem."

"You don't think we should be concerned about the Coast Guard?" Archie said, incredulity lifting her brows. "Not even a *little* concerned?"

"What, are you Alexander Hamilton's great-great-grandniece twice removed or something?" Houndstooth snapped. "It doesn't *matter*, Archie."

Cal sniffed, wiping his nose on his sleeve. "More important question: who's gonna light the fuses?"

Hero pulled two small black boxes out of their saddlebag, holding them aloft when Cal tried to grab one. "These," Hero said, "are remote detonation devices. I just push this button, and . . . boom."

Cal looked extremely dubious. "Hop shit," he said. "I've never heard of a *remote* detonator."

"That's because I invented them," Hero responded icily.

"I've seen them work," Houndstooth confirmed. He stared at Hero with an admiring smile. "They're amazing."

"Why two?" Archie asked. Hero smiled, enigmatic.

"Always have a backup plan, Archie."

Adelia stared at the map, her lips moving silently for a few moments. Then she frowned, her hands pressing against her belly. "This is a good plan. It will work, so long as you don't get eaten."

Houndstooth cleared his throat. "Hero will be riding Ruby while they set the charges." He said it with a hard look at Hero that spoke to many arguments over this decision. "Ruby can dodge the ferals' notice, and Travers', too."

Adelia glanced at him sharply. "We don't want this Travers to know what we are doing, is that right?"

Houndstooth nodded. "We'll be sticking to the islets, camping without a fire, laying low as we can. Until the job is done. We don't want to get on his bad side, Adelia. Travers is not a man whose eyes you want on you, if you're disrupting his business."

Adelia nodded as she rose from her crouch, rubbing her lower back. "He sounds dangerous. We should be vigilant." She grabbed her bedroll. "We should also be rested. Goodnight." Without another word, she stalked away from the fire. Archie caught Hero's eye, her brows raised. Hero shrugged in reply.

"She's right," Houndstooth said, rolling up the map. "We should sleep. We ride at dawn—we want to get through the Gate without drawing too much attention to ourselves."

Cal grabbed his bedroll, walking in the opposite direction from the one Adelia had chosen. "Five hoppers on six hippos," he said, loud enough to be heard by all the hoppers. "Shouldn't draw too much attention at all. Real subtle-like, this crew."

～

Adelia took the hippo's tusks during the night, presenting the cleaned and polished ivory to Archie before dawn.

"I couldn't sleep anyway," she said, bracing the small of her back, her eyes on the water. "The niña kicks me awake."

Archie watched the water, too, rather than watching

Adelia's face. Her eyes shone. "I suppose he's still at the bottom."

Adelia shrugged. "There are alligators here, I think. They would not bother us while we are riding, but who can say? I'm sure they get hungry, too."

Archie turned white and went back to polishing Rosa's saddle. Adelia stayed watching the water, chewing her lower lip, until Houndstooth's sharp whistle cut through the morning mist. They left the islet behind before the sun had finished rising. Not a one of them looked back.

~

The Gate was a thirteen-mile-long grate dividing the Harriet from the southern tip of the Mississippi River. It stood as a testament to Man's Victory over Nature—a brand seared into the landscape, marking it as the property of the federal government. It crossed the narrowest part of Louisiana's Mississippi River and extended inland by six and a half miles, just outside the overland range of all but the most determined ferals.

The openings in the grate were alligator-wide and fish-tall, designed by the finest engineers the government could subsidize to allow everything but boats, hippos, and law-abiding men to pass.

By the time the hoppers arrived at the Gate, the sun was

high and hot overhead, and all five of them were dewy with sweat. The Gate bowed toward them in places, the metal warped in the shape of rampaging feral bulls that had seen something worth having on the other side of the grate, but it was intact, and still looked strong. Debris floated in the water around the grate—sticks and leaves that hadn't been cleared by the crew of old soldiers who manned the outpost. Rosa picked through the water around the sticks, lifting her nose high in the air. Archie nudged her forward, peering at the grate. Ruby nosed at the sticks freely, searching for anything that appeared edible and ignoring Houndstooth entirely. Betsy, meanwhile, bowled through the flotsam, kicking up waves of water that soaked Cal to the waist and sent leaves flying at the other hoppers.

As they neared the outpost, they were greeted by the warning report of a rifle. A ranger peered down at them from one of the four high towers that dotted the thirteen-mile-long Gate, his face shaded by a broad-brimmed, sweat-stained hat with a Bureau of Land Management badge affixed to the brim.

"Alrigh' down there," he shouted. "Let's see your badges, just hold 'em high, now. No trouble."

Houndstooth produced a waxed wallet instead. He removed a large sheaf of paper and waved it in the air with one hand, cupping the other around his mouth.

"We don't have badges, but we have a contract with

the federal government. We've got free passage."

The ranger peered down at them, mopping his creased brow with a well-worn kerchief. Then, understanding bloomed across his face. "Are you the same Houndstooth what Alberto let through t'other day? Thought he told me you was a British fella."

"Yes, yes, that's me," Houndstooth called back up with a barely perceptible sigh. "Winslow Houndstooth, at your service, my good man. Would you terribly mind letting us through?"

The ranger spat brownly over the side of the Gate, well away from the five riders. "Sure enough, sure enough. Where'll you be staying?"

The voice that answered from beyond the Gate was smoother than a newborn hop's underbelly. "Not to worry, Harold. They'll be staying with me."

The ranger startled so violently that his hat fell off, dropping thirty feet from the tower. Hero caught it neatly, spinning it in their hands.

"Yes sir, Mr. Travers, sir," the ranger said, a quaver in his voice.

"Real subtle-like," Cal muttered to Houndstooth, his hand rising to touch the bandage over his left ear. Then he raised his voice, inclining his head toward the small, sleek man on the other side of the Gate. "Mr. Travers. What a fine surprise this is."

Chapter 9

TRAVERS RESTED COMFORTABLY in the center of his raft. He was surrounded on four sides by hulking men who trained rifles on the water, watching for ripples. "Calhoun. Mr. Houndstooth. Ladies." Hero made a disgruntled sound, and Mr. Travers tipped his hat to them in particular with a cough. "Et alia. I look forward to hosting you on the *Sturgess Queen*—my finest boat. Only the best accommodations."

"Oh, we couldn't possibly—" Hero began, but Mr. Travers interrupted.

"It's the least I can do in exchange for the immense services you'll be providing to the government of this great nation," he said with a thin smile. "I quite insist."

Houndstooth was still for a moment, his eyes on the goons' rifles. The Gate let out a ferocious squeal as the ranger pulled the lever to open it. It slid sideways, nesting neatly under the ranger's post. The wake lapped at the hippos' flanks, darkening the waxed leather of their harnesses.

"Well," Houndstooth said to the rest of the hoppers.

"I suppose it doesn't change too much if we're aboard the *Sturgess Queen*. Fewer fleas than the Inn, I'm sure." His face was open, and spoke to a pleasantly surprising change in plans. His expression betrayed none of the risk he was being forced to swallow. None of the rage.

It took a full minute for the Gate to open. The five of them walked through abreast, Zahra trailing behind Stasia. As they passed below the ranger's post, Hero flung the man's hat high in the air. It spun like a discus, and the ranger leaned out to catch it. The moment Zahra's tail had passed the threshold, the squeal began again, and the Gate closed behind them.

Behind Travers, the narrow passage of the Gate opened up into the waters of the Harriet. The humid haze of the day didn't quite obscure the massive dam that dominated the horizon behind him, dwarfing the river-boats and pleasure barges that dotted the water. Here and there, a canoe-sized islet bumped up out of the surface of the Harriet. Houndstooth would have expected them to be covered with birds—but then, he supposed the ferals made this a dangerous place to be a bird.

Mr. Travers clasped his hands in front of his chest, staring at the crew with wine-black eyes. His slim, slick moustache twitched over his icy smile. "Welcome to the Harriet."

~

Hero dropped their bag onto the floor of the presidential suite and took the room in. It was small as far as presidential suites went, but it was, according to Mr. Travers, the largest on the *Sturgess Queen.*

"Well," said Houndstooth. "Seems cozy enough, this. If you like red velvet." He ran a hand over the seat of the plush divan that sat under the window. Hero closed their eyes and breathed deeply. Their lips parted just a little, and Houndstooth nearly died with the effort of not noticing it.

"I do."

Houndstooth jumped. "What? You, hm, you what?"

Hero opened their eyes and considered Houndstooth, who was perched on the edge of the divan, stiff-backed, holding his hat in his lap. They cocked their head and smiled.

"I do like red velvet."

Houndstooth moved to the window and twitched the curtain aside. "What do you make of Travers, then? I don't like that he made us check our guns. 'Standard security procedures,' indeed. I don't like it. I don't like it at all. And did you see the munitions he had stored down there? What, is he expecting a war to break out?" He cleared his throat, smoothed the front of his jacket.

"I think," Hero drawled, crossing the room to join him, "that he's the least of our problems."

Hero stared out the window. Houndstooth stared at Hero. "What's the worst of our problems?"

Hero smiled, watching the water below them. "Well, Winslow. There's only one bed in here." They turned their head, still smiling, and took in Houndstooth's rich pink blush. "And last I counted, there's two of us."

Houndstooth stammered incoherently as Hero chucked him under the chin, then strolled out of the room, easing the door shut behind them. When the latch clicked, Houndstooth collapsed onto the divan. He stared at the bed, willing the heat to dissipate from his cheeks.

~

Archie and Adelia sat in the wood-paneled main lounge of the *Sturgess Queen*. Adelia's feet rested on a low, claw-footed stool. A glass of ice water sweated in her hand.

"They sure know how to treat a pregnant girl, eh?" She grinned over her glass at Archie, who sat in a wide wicker-backed armchair opposite her, turning the feral bull's tusk over and over in her hands.

"Why are you worried?" Adelia asked. "The worst thing that happens is they try to kill us."

Archie continued worrying at the tusk. She muttered something under her breath.

"Que?"

"I said," Archie replied deliberately, "that I'm not sure it's them I'm worried about."

"What do you mean?"

"I mean they knew that we would be getting to the Gate today. They knew 'ow many of us to expect. They 'ad exactly six spots in the paddock, one for each 'ippo. And they 'ad enough rooms set aside for six people, which means they knew about . . . about Neville."

"So?"

"So," Archie said, her hands going still, "I think that someone told them about us. I think that someone told them what route we would be taking. I think—"

"What's all this about?" Hero said, striding into the lounge.

"Archie thinks that we have a spy in our midst," Adelia said with a crooked grin. Hero looked sharply at Archie.

"A spy?"

"Oui," Archie replied, her brows high. "I inspected the Gate while 'oundstooth was talking to that 'illbilly ranger. It was sturdy, intact, no recent welding that I could see. And we all know that a 'ippo isn't going to reach higher ramming speeds overland than in the water."

"What's your point, Archie?" Hero asked, not unkindly.

"My point is: if the Gate was not broken, then 'ow exactly did a single feral bull escape the Harriet and find us? Just the one? Not enough for us to notice and change course? I'll tell you how: Monsieur Travers snapped 'is fingers, and that guard let it out. I'd guess that 'appened on the same day we 'it the road. The only question is, who was gone long enough to send a telegram?"

Adelia, Archie, and Hero looked at each other. None of them wanted to be the first to speak.

The doors to the lounge swung open, and Houndstooth strode in briskly. "Well! Why the long faces, you three? And where's Calhoun?"

Adelia rattled the ice in her glass. "I'd imagine 'e's at the blackjack tables," she said, plucking out an ice cube and pressing it to her neck. "Ay, it's too hot."

"You alright, Adelia?" Hero asked.

"Si, si, it's just—nobody ever told me that having a little girl would make me so hot all the time!"

Houndstooth, being a gentleman, said nothing; he kept his eyes averted from Adelia's ripe belly. Hero, having no such compunctions, laughed heartily. "Get used to it, ma'am. We have a saying where I'm from—boys will make you cry, but girls? Girls will make you sweat."

~

The lamps that lit the riverboat inside and out had come on by the time Archie found Cal on the casino floor. He swayed gently on his stool, and it was readily apparent that bourbon, rather than the rocking rhythm of the boat, was what moved him. Archie pulled up a stool beside him and mentally tallied the cash that rested in stacks on his side of the felt.

"'Ow are you doing, there, mon ami?" she asked softly. Cal swung his head around to her and grinned broadly. Blood was seeping through the bandage over his left ear. He had two toothpicks in his mouth. One was fresh; the other was chewed nearly to splinters, as though he'd forgotten to discard the old one.

"Archie! Or should I say, *Regina*?" He leered as he said her name, and she thought she could guess what pun he thought he was making.

"Actually, cherie, it's Regina. Rhymes with Pasadena."

His leer dissolved, and he became morose so quickly that Archie feared he would fall off his stool.

"You know Pasadena, oui, Calhoun? That is where you met our Adelia—on a supply trip for Mr. 'oundstooth, was it not? A decade ago, oui?"

"I don't wanna talk about Adelia," Cal slurred. "I miss Adelia so—" He hiccupped. "—so much, and I don't wanna talk about her. She won'—she won' even talk to me about the baby, Regina. After what I did for her? She came back to me and then, and then she left, an'—I don't wanna talk about her, no, no thank you."

"Ah, of course, of course—" Cal interrupted Archie before she could finish agreeing not to talk about Adelia.

"I met 'er in Pasadena, you know," he said, having already apparently forgotten that Archie had said just that a few moments before. "I met 'er there and I loved—I loved her right away. I was so nice to her, but she just wouldn't even *lookuhme*." He slapped the table with the palm of his hand. "Wouldn't go home with a ranch hand, no sir. Too good for *that*!" His too-loud voice suddenly wobbled. "Too good for *me*. But I showed her, I did everything he asked me to do and *then some*—"

Other patrons of the *Sturgess Queen*'s bar were starting to stare. Archie put a hand on Cal's elbow. "Perhaps we should get you to bed, non? It would appear that you are winning. Best to quit while you are ahead, is it not?"

Cal shook his finger at her, squinting. "Not yet," he said in a stage whisper. "Not yet. I'm not done yet." He turned back to the dealer, who had observed this exchange with the removed patience of experience, and slapped the felt hard enough that one of his stacks of cash fell over. He left his hand where it lay, and his gaze swam up to meet the dealer's eyes. "Himme."

The dealer did as he was told, and Archie saw at once that she should not have allowed Cal to touch the table.

"Twenty-one. Again. Excellent, Mr. Hotchkiss." The dealer smiled at Cal, but his smile did not extend to his eyes. He moved his hand as though to shift more cash to Cal's side of the table, but at the last moment, he seized Cal's wrist instead.

Archie sprang from her stool, her hand going automatically to her empty holster, as the dealer gripped Cal's wrist and waved his other hand in a signal. Mr. Travers appeared as though from thin air, his hands clasped soberly behind his back.

"Well now, Mr. Hotchkiss. What have you been up to?"

The dealer lifted Cal's hand, revealing a single card underneath it.

"This is the fourth card he's swapped, Mr. Travers, sir. I wasn't sure at first, but, well." The dealer smiled at the small army of empty highball glasses that littered the table. "He got sloppy."

Cal looked from the dealer to Travers' unsmiling face, and then to Archie. His expression was that of a boy who has fallen into a well at dusk, and who has yelled himself hoarse with no answer but the rustle of wind through buzzards' wings.

"Mr. Hotchkiss," Travers said, reaching into his breast

pocket and pulling out a bloody, folded pocket square. "I believe you'll be needing this back." He tucked the pocket square into Cal's shirt pocket. Cal blanched and started muttering the word "no" under his breath, over and over, like an incantation.

"Mr. Travers, sir, Cal is drunk. Might I take 'im up to his room to sleep this off? He is not 'imself." Archie's voice was dripping honey. Travers regarded her with frank interest.

"Why, Miss Archambault. It is so refreshing to see someone willing to stick up for a friend. But I'm afraid that Mr. Hotchkiss here is a cheat. Ah, ah—" He held up a finger, cutting off her interruption. "He may be drunk, but he is still a cheat. He was a cheat before he was drunk and he'll remain a cheat when he sobers up tomorrow." He took a step away from Cal. The dealer did the same.

Cal bolted for the door. The band stopped playing to watch him pass. He was fast—but Travers' security goons were faster. They caught him under the arms midstride, hauling him into the air with the brisk efficiency and remorselessness of experience.

"No!" he cried, his legs kicking in the air but finding no purchase as he was dragged bodily across the casino floor. "No, wait, Mr. Travers, sir, please! You can't, you can't—after what I did for you? After what I did to that

British bastard for you? Please, sir, I won't—I wasn't—"

Travers laid his fingertips on Archie's arm, as though to comfort her. "Watch now."

And she did. She watched as Travers' men paused at the window. Cal's eyes roamed the room, sightless with terror. He screamed. He begged.

Travers' men did not seem to hear. They swung him once—heave-ho, and his toothpicks fell to the floor—then hurled him bodily through the open window.

He screamed as he fell; the splash seemed to echo in the silent casino. Then, he screamed again. It was not a scream of terror, but a scream of pain.

After a moment, the screaming stopped—but the splashing continued.

Travers clapped his hands once in front of his chest, then addressed the now-silent patrons who filled the gambling tables of his casino. "Ladies and gentlemen, my apologies for the disruption!" He turned to the bar. "To make up for it, a round of champagne for everyone, on the house!"

Travers signaled the band, and the music started playing once again. He laid his fingertips lightly upon Archie's arm once more as the casino floor erupted in cheers.

"I hope, Miss Archambault, that you can understand. Mr. Hotchkiss was a thief, and I cannot abide thieves."

His use of the past tense was not lost on Archie. "I, of course, would not even *begin* to consider allowing his shortcomings to color my opinions of the rest of your little hopper gang."

Archie managed a smile, and touched his fingertips with her own. "I . . . I am so grateful, Mr. Travers. We 'ad no idea that Cal—" But she saw his wry, knowing smile and started again. "Of course, we knew that he was a scoundrel, but we would never imagine that he would besmirch your 'ospitality so."

"Of course not, Miss Archambault. Of course not." A waiter approached holding a silver tray of glasses, and Travers handed one to Archie before taking one for himself. He touched his glass to hers, making the crystal sing.

"Cheers, Miss Archambault. May you enjoy your stay on the *Sturgess Queen,* and the very best of luck in all your endeavors."

"Santé," Archie answered, and drained her glass without looking away from Travers' twinkling eyes. Travers signaled the band to play louder, and they did—but the music couldn't mask the bellowing of the ferals fighting over their feast in the river below.

Chapter 10

"I'M NOT SURE I UNDERSTAND what you mean, Archie." Houndstooth's voice was low. If Archie hadn't known better, she'd have thought he was furious. But she did know better—she'd saved the man's life somewhere between nine and a half and ten times, and she knew his moods better than her own.

So she knew that he was perched on the edge of panic.

"Dead means dead, mon ami. Nothing more to it."

Houndstooth ran his hands through his hair as he paced back and forth, staring at the carpet. Hero, seated on the divan, followed him with their eyes. "But . . . but if he's dead, then—then I can't—then I didn't—"

Archie put a quelling hand on his shoulder. "Perhaps it is best this way, non?" she whispered. "Without the revenge."

He looked up at her, his eyes flashing. "How did you know?"

She looked uncomfortable. Before she had to answer—before she had to tell him what Cal had said just before he died—the door banged open. Adelia stared in at the two of them. "Well, Archie. I suppose this means you and I each get our own suite."

"It also means we're all up to our necks in the bog without so much as a hop to ride," Houndstooth said in a clipped voice. "We can't do this without Cal." He began to pace the suite, running his hands through his hair.

Hero didn't look up from their whittling. "If you're so beside yourself about it, Winslow, I can chew on toothpicks and sling racial slurs with the best of 'em. Might need to practice some, but I'm sure I can get in fightin' shape by mornin'."

Houndstooth laughed—a genuine, easy laugh—and then sat heavily on the bed next to Archie.

"Look around the room, Hero. What's missing?"

Hero glanced around the suite. "Palpable body odor."

Houndstooth laughed again, but this time, the laugh seemed forced. Adelia and Archie exchanged a glance.

"We're missing a white boy," Adelia murmured, stroking her belly.

"So what?" Archie huffed. "If we need one so bad, I am sure I can drag one back up here for you, Winslow. There's no shortage."

Houndstooth was staring at Hero. Hero stared back at him for a long moment.

"What is it? What are we failing to understand here, Winslow? What's so tough about pulling off this hippo caper without Cal on board?"

Houndstooth dropped his head into his hands. "We need your supplies, Hero. And nobody on the Harriet is going to sell your supplies to a stranger, not even for easy money. We've been corresponding with a dealer and he's expecting Cal to come buy the goods from him, and we're working with him on the strength of Cal's reputation on the Harriet. He's expecting Cal. He's expecting a white man with a terrible mistake of a moustache." He rubbed his face with his hands, groaning. "And it's *not a caper*; it's an *operation*."

Hero whittled faster, sending hickory shavings flying into the plush red carpet. "Right, right. All aboveboard. So, ask your federal boy. I'm sure the army can send something."

Houndstooth looked uncomfortable. "I can't ask him."

Hero's lips quirked into a half smile. "Oh, honestly. You're *embarrassed*?"

Houndstooth scowled at them. "No, I'm not *embarrassed*, it's just that—he doesn't know what we're going to do, here. He's assuming we'll net each feral, one by one, and escort them out of the swamp. That's why the contract is for a full *year*."

Adelia swore under her breath. "That's . . . idiotic."

"That's dangerous," Archie added.

"That's why we're not doing it that way," Houndstooth

said. Houndstooth slapped the edge of the map, his cheeks pink. "It was a great goddamned plan, and it's *sunk*." Hero put a calming hand on his arm. His cheeks reddened further.

"So we need a white boy por quoi? To buy dynamite?"

Hero nodded. "Lots of it. And detonators. Fuses, timers—oh, and wax. A lot of wax."

Archie left the room without saying another word.

"Where is she going?" Adelia asked.

"Probably to go charm some poor kid into buying Hero's groceries," Houndstooth replied. "I suppose that's why she's on the team—she could talk a hippo into thinking it was a rhinoceros without breaking a sweat."

A few minutes later, the door burst open again. Adelia smirked.

"Giving up so soon, eh Ar—oh," she said.

Archie stood in the doorway, transformed. She'd slicked her hair down on either side of a part so razor sharp it put Houndstooth's to shame. Her pinstriped breeches and satin waistcoat had been exchanged for a flawlessly tailored three-piece linen suit. She spun a matching bowler hat between her hands. Her boots were half-covered by diamond-white spats. A blond moustache—one that would have kept Cal up at night with envy—bristled its way across her upper lip.

She had become an impeccably outfitted gentleman.

"You needed a white boy, oui?" she asked, her voice pitched an octave lower than usual. "Et voilà."

Houndstooth gaped at her as Hero crossed the room to examine her. "Where did you get this suit?" Hero asked. "I don't mean any offense, but I can't imagine you just grabbed it off some poor mark in the hallway just now. And that moustache—good God, Archie, it's nothing like Cal's, but it'll *do*!"

"I keep it around for special occasions," Archie replied with a grin. "Sometimes my heart calls more to suits than skirts. It is fluid, oui?" She waved her hand vaguely through the air. "It changes. The tailor, 'e was confused when I told 'im what I wanted, but for the right price, anything can be 'ad. Isn't that right, Adelia?"

Adelia's head snapped up from where she was staring at the map. "Que?"

Houndstooth seemed to come to his senses. "Archie, you . . . you brilliant woman, I could kiss you!"

Archie and Hero both scowled. "You will ruin my moustache, 'oundstooth. Best to keep that kiss for someone who wants it, eh?" She placed the bowler hat on her head and turned to Hero, whose eyes went wide.

"Do you 'ave a list for me?"

"A list? Oh! A list. Of course, yes, let me just—" Hero scrambled for paper and scrawled out a list of supplies, handing it to Archie.

"Well, my friends, off I go. I expect all three of you to be drunk at the bar by the time I return." She tipped a wink at Hero. "We must make a good show of enjoying our stay on the *Sturgess Queen,* non?"

~

Archie didn't return until the wee hours of the morning. As she and Rosa approached the dock, she looked around at the Harriet. She hadn't really paid attention to it the day before—she had been more focused on the guns Travers' goons were carrying. Through the night, it had been too dark to really take in. As the sky began to lighten, she realized that the Harriet was precisely what she had expected: a huge, flat, muddy stretch of water, dotted with tiny islets and bracketed by humps of dogwood-covered land. She found herself wishing it was more beautiful, more shaded and lush—but then, she thought, it would be good marshland for hippos rather than a prison for ferals and riverboat thugs.

She unloaded Rosa's saddlebags onto the floating dock that bridged the gap between the *Sturgess Queen* and the paddock. She brushed Rosa's teeth and put medicated drops into the albino hippo's pink eyes. Then, she sang Rosa a short lullaby and began dragging her load aboard the boat.

She tapped on the door to Hero and Houndstooth's cabin with one fingernail, then with two. When there was no answer, she gave a single rap on the door with her knuckle.

Hero answered the door, breathless, still tying the belt of a robe around their waist. Their eyes were glassy—their lips, swollen. Archie grinned wickedly.

"I'm glad to see you, too, 'ero." She thrust the saddlebag at Hero and turned to leave.

"Wait," Hero panted. "Wait, this isn't—this can't be enough. I need at least four times this much dynamite."

Archie turned back, her eyes still glinting with delight. "Ah, well, you see. They were all out of dynamite." She patted the top of the bulging saddlebag. "This is something different. Something . . . better. You'll see. We will discuss it further in the morning, oui? You're busy now, and I'm so very sleepy." She yawned theatrically. "Off to bed with both of us, is it not?"

She sauntered away down the hallway, pulling off the false moustache. "Oh, 'oundstooth," she murmured to herself, a smile overtaking her face as she remembered the longing look on Winslow's face when Hero had touched his arm the day before. "I can't save you this time, mon copain. You're done for."

~

Archie, Hero, and Houndstooth met in the lounge at noon, each of them still blinking sleep from their eyes. Adelia was already seated in her chair, a small armory's worth of freshly whetted knives on a table by her side. The knife she was sliding along the whetstone was familiar; Archie noticed it before Houndstooth did.

"I thought that thing was lodged too deep in the bull's brain to get out? And—'ow did you get those back from Travers? I thought they were all locked away . . . ?"

Adelia grinned and continued sharpening Houndstooth's ivory-handled blade. "I'm determined, Archie. Determination is everything. Besides, I had a few years of saving Cal's pistol-ridden ass. You know how it is, in the water."

Archie watched Adelia's expert hands work. "I do know 'ow it is. Knives are a 'opper's best friend. Pistols that can't get wet, on the other 'and? A nightmare."

Adelia laughed. "Well, Cal was an idiot, wasn't he? I told him, a hopper with no knives is a dead hopper. But he didn't want to listen." She lowered her voice in a perfect imitation of Cal. "'Well, actually, Adelia, a gun is more effective at a distance.' See how well that worked out for him, hm?"

Hero and Houndstooth walked to the dining room for coffee, their heads tilted toward each other as they walked. Archie sat across from Adelia, her elbows resting on her knees.

"Adelia, mind if I ask you a question?"

Adelia did not look up from the knife. "Yes. It's Cal's baby. No, I am not sorry that he's dead."

Archie shifted uncomfortably. "Well, that's . . . that's good to know, but it's not what I was going to ask."

That made Adelia look up. Her face was, for the first time, completely open—Archie realized she had not seen plain emotion on the woman's face before.

"What would you like to know, Archie?"

"I don't mean any offense, of course—you are incredibly skilled, obviously you are an asset. But . . . why are you 'ere?"

Adelia's face split into a wide, white smile. Archie realized that one of Adelia's canines was made of gold, and she was reminded strongly of Ruby's deadly sharp tusks.

"Why, Archie. I'm here to kill you."

Archie was startled into laughter. Adelia went back to sharpening Houndstooth's knife. She tested it against her thumbnail, then returned it to the whetstone.

"What? Me?"

"Well, not *you* precisely. But, all of you. Everyone on the team."

Archie went very still. "I think perhaps I misunderstand your joke, madame."

"Oh, it's not a joke," Adelia said, although her smile had not faltered. "I'm here to kill you all. If anyone goes rogue, if anyone tries to steal the money, if anyone sabotages the plan. I'm supposed to keep an eye on you, per the boss."

"You mean the Bureau of Land Management? Or 'oundstooth?"

Adelia did not reply.

"Aha," Archie said. "So you're keeping an eye on us for this 'boss' of yours. But who keeps their eye on *you*, Adelia Reyes?"

Archie stood after a long, silent moment, and walked into the dining room after Houndstooth and Hero. Adelia watched her go, testing the knife on her thumbnail once more. This time, she found it more than sharp enough.

Chapter 11

THEY MET THE NEXT DAY in Hero and Houndstooth's suite to assemble the bombs that would drive the ferals to the Gate.

"So," Hero said, staring into Archie's saddlebag.

"The man I bought it from, Mr. Wolffenstein? 'E said you would know what it is. 'E called it 'the Mother of Satan'?"

"Madre del Diablo?" Adelia asked. "I've heard of that before, I think. But I thought it was just a *rumor*."

Hero took a rapid step away from the saddlebag. "No, no, it's not a rumor at all, Adelia. Triacetone triperoxide." They aimed a pointed look at Archie. "It's *extremely* volatile."

Archie shrugged. "Wolffenstein said it was so pure that it could be considered relatively stable."

Hero pulled a single tiny white crystal out of the saddlebag and threw it to the ground. It exploded with a loud pop.

" . . .'e said *relatively*," Archie said with a shrug.

"Well then *you* can be the one to handle it," Hero

replied. "I hope you brought gloves."

Archie pulled a pair of long leather gloves from the back pocket of her green breeches. "'Ero, darling, I *always* bring gloves."

For the remainder of the afternoon, Adelia sat cross-legged on the divan, massaging wax into leather pouches, rendering them effectively waterproof. Archie filled each wallet with the tiny white crystals of madre del Diablo, then handed each one to Hero, who inserted wires and bits of metal in a configuration that seemed to make sense to them and them alone. Archie asked what Hero was doing, and the response was in no way illuminating.

"Would you like to discuss the inner workings of a blasting cap, Archie? Because we can discuss the inner workings of a blasting cap, if that's what you're looking for here."

Archie had groaned and shoved Hero's shoulder. "If you don't want to tell me, then don't tell me." Hero had grinned and gone back to work, and Archie had caught Houndstooth beaming at them.

After Hero had finished doing whatever it was they were doing to make the bombs sufficiently dangerous, they wrapped each leather pouch around itself a few times. There was more room than they needed, since the crystals were so much smaller and lighter than the dynamite Hero had been expecting.

"You've worked out the equivalency, I suppose?" Houndstooth asked.

"More or less," Hero replied. "We might get a little bigger bang than we expected, but I think it'll all even out in the end. Don't worry, Houndstooth. This hippo caper will go off without a hitch."

Houndstooth opened his mouth to reply, and they all responded with him: "It's *not a caper;* it's an *operation.*"

The final step was left to Houndstooth. He had a pot of melted wax, kept liquid by water boiled in his travel kettle—Adelia had rolled her eyes at him for bringing it, but there wasn't an inn north of Lafayette that could brew an acceptable pot of tea. He sealed each leather pouch, pouring wax over the seams.

After the first one was finished, he held it up. It was about the size of both his hands, and didn't look remotely dangerous.

"Are you certain that this will be enough of a bang, Hero?"

Hero looked up at him with a half smile. "I think I know how to create a *bang,* Houndstooth."

Houndstooth's ears turned violet, and he didn't speak again until they had finished making all twenty bombs.

~

That evening, Hero prepared to ride into the Harriet to set up the bombs. Houndstooth accompanied them to the dock at dusk, carrying one of the two loaded saddle-bags that they'd need to take out onto the water.

"Now, remember, don't place the charges too close—"

"Too close to the dam, I know. You've only told me a thousand times, Winslow." Hero smiled. "I know the dam has a crack. I know we don't want to be the ones to blow it. Trust me, why don't you?"

Abigail waited for Hero dockside, impatient. She blew bubbles in the water when she saw them approaching. Houndstooth looked at her apologetically, then whistled for Ruby, who slipped up to the dock like butter sliding across the bottom of a hot pan.

"You don't have to go alone, you know," Houndstooth said, dropping his saddlebag.

Hero regarded him with their steady gaze. "Oh, Winslow. If I didn't know better, I'd think you were worried about me."

Houndstooth rubbed the back of his neck. "Maybe I just want to go with you. Keep you company."

Hero dropped their saddlebag beside his, taking his hand. "Or maybe you don't know how to stay behind?" Houndstooth grimaced at the insight. "I'll be with Ruby. You can't come with me, not riding Abigail—she's louder in the water than a passel of fighting alligators, and if she sees ferals, she'll probably try to make friends. Besides, you need to stay here. If Travers catches wind of this . . . you can say I went rogue, that you didn't know I had this planned. You can say that the whole idea was to get the hippos out one at a time, nice and slow, like they thought. If they catch both of us, though—it would be bad for everyone, Houndstooth. You know that." Hero kept going before Houndstooth could interrupt them. "Plus, you've got to dispose of the rest of the madre del Diablo—it only took about half of what Archie brought to get us set up, and we don't want to leave that stuff lying around."

Houndstooth was silent for a long moment, staring at Hero's face as though trying to find a constellation in a sea of stars. "I wish you weren't so damnably *brilliant,* Hero. You've thought of everything, haven't you?" He touched Hero's face with a tentative hand. "You'll be a hero, Hero. If this works. You'll be a *hero.* I just don't want you to be a *dead* hero."

"I'll be fine," Hero said, smiling. "Ruby's the best there is. She won't let anything happen to me. You can trust her, and you can trust me. You don't have to w—"

But Hero's words were stopped by Houndstooth's mouth on theirs, his hands on their waist. "I do trust you, you know," he whispered against their lips—and just like that, there was nothing left to say.

~

Adelia found Houndstooth at the bar half an hour later. He was already half drunk, and well on his way to getting whole drunk, if the speed at which he gulped his whiskey meant anything.

"Mind if I join you?" she said, hoisting herself onto a bar stool.

"Of course, please do," he said politely, signaling the bartender to get her a glass of water.

"Ever the gentleman."

"Ever the Englishman, you mean," he replied, speaking into his nearly empty glass.

Adelia handed Houndstooth the ivory-handled knife. "Here—cleaned and sharpened. Sorry for, you know." She gestured to his jacket pocket, wiggling her fingers. "Reaching in there, like that. Without asking first."

Houndstooth turned the knife in his hand a few times, examining the blade. "It looks better than it has since I got it. You have a gift, Adelia."

She smiled. "I suppose you could say I have the touch." She sipped her water. "You left England to open a ranch here in the States, didn't you, Houndstooth?"

He nodded. "Left home for good when I was fifteen. It was all I wanted. I didn't know any better."

"Do you miss it?"

"What? England? Every day. And, not at all. They didn't like me there, you know," he said, swaying a little on his bar stool. "They didn't like a damn thing about me, other than my name."

Adelia laughed. "I meant being a rancher. You used to own a ranch, sì? You used to breed your very own, like Ruby." She put a hand on his arm, steadying him, then quickly withdrew her hand.

Houndstooth signaled for another drink. "I'd rather not discuss it, if you don't mind. It ended . . . badly. And I am, after all, English. We don't like to *discuss*."

"It's okay," she said, resting a hand on her belly. "I actually already know about what happened. About the fire. Cal told me." She watched Houndstooth closely. He stared into the glass of brown liquor that appeared in front of him.

"Did he now?" he murmured to the whiskey. "Did he tell you?"

Adelia waited.

"Did he tell you?" Houndstooth repeated. "Did he tell you about who burned down my ranch? Did he tell you about why he hid on the Harriet for all these years, knowing Travers wouldn't let me in? Oh, he knew," Houndstooth said, mistaking Adelia's stillness for doubt. "Travers would never let me through the Gate. I turned him down when he asked me to help introduce more vicious strains into the feral population. He spent years trying to change my mind, but I wouldn't budge. Frankly, I'm surprised he didn't burn my ranch down himself—" He glanced over at Adelia, understanding dawning across his face. She interrupted, talking fast and low.

"Don't you ever wish you could go back to it, Houndstooth? Just . . . leave this place, give up the capers, give up the vendetta? Just take the money and run?"

He stared at her, his brow knit. "Run?"

"You know." She made a shooing motion with her hands. *"Leave."*

He shook his head, and it made him sway hard. "I can't just—"

She grabbed his face in both hands, steadying him. She looked into his eyes with urgent intensity—he feared for a moment that she was going to try to kiss him. She hissed through her teeth. "Forget what you came here to do, Houndstooth. Forget revenge. *Leave. Leave tonight.*"

"'Oundstooth, you rascal, I 'ave been looking for you everywhere!" Archie's voice filled the bar, and Adelia jumped away from Houndstooth. He looked at her as though she'd suddenly grown hippo ears, bewilderment writ plain across his normally stoic Englishman's face. Archie stood in the doorway, beaming, and walked toward them.

"Adelia, ma nénette, 'ow are you feeling? Do your feet

pain you at the end of such a long day? Ah, I thought they might, so I asked the bellboy to prepare you a soak of warm water and lavender in the lounge." Ignoring Adelia's protests, Archie helped her down from the barstool and began walking her toward the lounge. "I asked 'im to bring a little glass of wine with honey in it, to settle the bébé." Her voice was as bright as the edge of a freshly sharpened knife. "I know she 'as been kicking you *right in the gut* these past few days."

They rounded the corner to the lounge, leaving Houndstooth to stare, lost, into his whiskey at the bar. The moment he was out of sight, Archie rounded on Adelia, sticking a finger into her face.

"What the hell do you think you are doing?"

Adelia's nostrils flared. She jutted her jaw toward Archie, saying, "It's called *flirting*."

Archie snorted. "I would 'ardly call it anything that advanced. What are you thinking? For the first time in the ten years I've known 'im, 'e likes someone who's worth 'is time. You stay out of it, Adelia." Archie's eyes went wide with surprise as she registered pain in her side.

"I'd gut you right here, if I didn't think he'd jump on the blade right after you," Adelia whispered. Her knife dug into Archie's side, the point of it pressed between her ribs. "If there's one thing I know about Winslow Houndstooth, it is that he cannot be tied down, no matter how much he 'likes' the latest flower he's landed on." An ugly, brittle smile crept across her face. "Just because he wouldn't have you—"

Archie cut her off with a laugh. "'E's not my type, cherie. Put your knife away. You're embarrassing yourself, even more 'ere than you were at the bar." She took a deft step away from Adelia's blade, and turned to walk back into the bar. "Try to calm yourself down, eh?" She called over her shoulder. "I think the baby is making you crazy."

Adelia stared after her. Archie's voice drifted back to her from the bar—"Ah, Houndstooth, right where I left you! 'Ow about some water to befriend the whiskey in your belly, eh? You should be keeping your wits about you during our big caper."

"It's not a *caper*—" came the weary reply.

Adelia looked down at the knife in her hand; a drop of Archie's blood fell from the tip of the blade to the plush red carpet at her feet. It blended right in.

"Well, well, well. Miss Reyes," came a smooth, sleek voice from the shadows of the lounge. "What on earth have you been up to?"

~

Hero finished rigging the bombs in the wee hours of the morning. They were pleased by the simplicity of the setup; each one of the waxed-leather wallets was fixed to the top of an existing buoy in the Harriet, keeping them safe from accidental bumps and early detonation. The wax was a precaution—one never knew what might happen to a buoy during a stampede of ferals—but Hero felt fairly confident that the risk of immersion was low, and that the chances of success were incredibly high.

As they nudged Ruby toward the floating dock next to the hippo paddock of the *Sturgess Queen,* Hero raised one hand to their lips, and felt a smile lingering there. Houndstooth. He had a reputation—every one of the hoppers on this team had a reputation—but he had turned out to be so much more than an English snob with a taste for pretty eyes. Hero wondered what would happen when the job was over—would they go home together, to Hero's little house with its little pond? Retirement alone had been dull, and lonely, and not the respite they'd so needed. But what if Houndstooth were there? Maybe sitting on the porch and drinking sweet tea and watching the fireflies come out wouldn't be such a lonesome proposition anymore. Maybe it would be the peaceful retirement they'd been hoping for when they bought the little house with the little pond.

Maybe, Hero thought, closing the paddock Gate and turning Ruby loose.

Maybe.

They walked up the dock, exhausted, and walked into the entryway of the *Sturgess Queen*. Upstairs, they knew, Houndstooth would still be awake, watching the window for their return. They could sleep beside him for a few hours, before it was time for the action to begin.

To Hero's surprise, there were voices in the lounge. The *Sturgess Queen was* supposed to be empty during the night—all the gamblers and drinkers headed to the Inn or to one of Travers' pleasure barges to recover from their losses and their headaches. The voices that Hero heard weren't shouting over a craps table, though. They were soft ones—voices that didn't want to be heard. Hero paused at the foot of the stairs when they heard a familiar accent drifting through the doorway.

"Their plan will work. And it will work quickly. It's going to happen today—the ferals will be gone by nightfall."

Adelia. The skin on the back of Hero's neck prickled.

"Oh, *Adelia*. Did you even *try* to seduce the Englishman?" The voice that answered Adelia was rich, smooth. Slick. *Travers*. Hero swore under their breath. *Archie was right.*

"I told you, I don't do seduction. Besides, the French one got in the way, and I—"

"Ah, excuses. I—that knife would be put to better use elsewhere, Miss Reyes," came Travers' reply. "In Miss Archambault's heart, for example? In Mr. Houndstooth's gullet?" Hero covered their mouth with both hands as Travers suggested ways to kill the hoppers with all the insouciance of a maître d' reading off the specials.

"The time for manipulation and the arrangement of coincidences is over, Adelia," Travers continued, his voice growing cool. "I've been willing to work with you to maintain your illusion of camaraderie, but now we do things my way." A creak and a rustle of cloth. "I have business to attend to out on the water tonight. Find me back here before noon. Bring Houndstooth's tongue with you as proof that you've done your job. No ears or toes, do you understand? That's a good girl."

Hero heard Adelia shout something that had the cadence of a vicious epithet. A door slammed—one or both of them leaving the room via a different entrance. Hero immediately turned to creep up the stairs to their room, each step cautious and silent. They moved slowly, trying to keep the boat from creaking under the weight of their footfalls.

They had to tell Houndstooth. They had to tell him, and they had to do—what? Something. Anything.

But then the door behind them swung open, and it was too late.

Adelia's face was already contorted with restrained rage from her conversation with Travers. When she saw

Hero standing there, so close to the door to the lounge that it was impossible for them not to have heard everything, her expression dropped into something like relief.

"Hero," she said, a slow smile spreading across her lips. "I suppose you've finished rigging the bombs? I suppose you haven't been up to tell Houndstooth that you were successful? I suppose you just wanted a word, before you go up to bed?"

Hero took several steps backward, but they were too late to dodge Adelia's lightning-quick knives. They didn't even see her hand move before they felt the pain in their gut. Hero dropped their hands to the hilt of the knife that protruded from their belly like the stump of a silvery umbilicus.

"I—"

Before they could so much as begin making an appeal to Adelia—an appeal for what? For mercy? Surely it was too late for that—Hero felt a blow strike them in the chest, like a punch. And there, like magic, the hilt of another knife had sprouted from their chest.

Hero fell to the plush red carpet of the entryway, at the bottom of the stairs. They looked up the stairs, away from Adelia, toward the suite where Houndstooth was waiting for them. They wanted to scream, to shout, to warn him—but it was so hard to draw breath. They hiccupped with pain, and tasted copper. They fought; they strug-

gled, and managed to draw a single lungful of air.

"No no, dulce Hero. Sin gritando." Adelia's whisper was right next to Hero's ear. The last thing Hero saw before they passed out was Houndstooth, standing at the top of the stairs, his mouth open in a scream to answer the one for which Hero had been unable to find breath.

Chapter 12

ARCHIE SAT ON THE DIVAN and watched Houndstooth pace.

"Cherie, you should 'ave a drink. Sit down. Something. You are driving me crazy with this pacing."

"I can't sit down. Not until we decide what to do with *her*."

Adelia sat in the high-backed chair, bound by lashings of rope. Her head lolled to one side. A significant bruise marred her head where Archie had struck her with a well-flung hammer strike as she had attempted to run away from Hero's still body.

Hero lay on the bed, their breathing ragged, their wounds packed with the torn scraps of one of Houndstooth's silk shirts. The wounds had not been shallow, but Hero's sternum had stopped Adelia's knife from hitting their heart, and the blood pouring from their belly had slowed just enough to give Houndstooth a shiver of hope.

"You're certain she's been spying?" Houndstooth asked Archie for the hundredth time. Archie lifted a handful of papers she'd found in Adelia's belongings: a contract, signed in Adelia's loopy cursive and Travers' delicate calligraphy.

"'Oundstooth? 'Oundstooth. *Winslow Remington 'oundstooth, look at me,*" Archie commanded. Houndstooth stopped and obeyed, staring at her with lost eyes, his hands limp by his sides.

"We 'ave to kill her, 'oundstooth. We 'ave to kill her and then we 'ave to run. Now. Tonight."

"Leaving, are you?" came a low drawl from the doorway. They hadn't heard Gran Carter enter, but there he was, leaning against the doorframe: six feet three inches of coiled muscle. His hands were nowhere near the two six-shooters that dangled from his hips, but Houndstooth and Archie both froze as though he were pointing the guns directly at them.

"I don't believe we've had the pleasure, Mr. Houndstooth." He extended his hand to Houndstooth, who shook it out of sheer reflex. "Gran Carter, U.S. marshal. You have something I've been looking for." He tipped his black hat at Archie. "Good to see you again, Archie. How've you been?"

"I 'ave been well, Gran. I 'ave been . . . busy. I'm sorry I 'aven't written." Archie sounded like she meant it.

"Oh, that's fine. I know how time gets away from you." He took a small step toward her, a smile twitching at the corners of this mouth. "I've missed you."

Archie looked at her hands, worrying at the contract that sat in her lap. "Now is not the time, Gran."

Gran cleared his throat, looking to Houndstooth. "Mr. Houndstooth. I believe you're in charge of this hippo caper?"

Houndstooth looked simultaneously pained and affronted. "It's not a caper, Mr. Carter." Behind him, Archie mouthed the words along with him. "It's an *operation,* all aboveboard. We were hired by the federal government, I'll have you know, and—"

"Oh, my apologies, Mr. Houndstooth. I misspoke. *Of course* it only makes sense that the federal government of the United States of America would hire a team of down-and-out criminals for a caper on the Harriet."

"It's not a *caper*—"

"Yes, well. At any rate." Carter grinned at Archie. "Miss Reyes is none of your concern. She's hardly a member of your crew at this point, is she?"

Houndstooth seemed uncertain as to how he should respond. Adelia had been a member of the crew until thirty minutes before; but now, with Hero's blood on her hands?

"I'll make this easy," Carter said, with the same relaxed grin. "Miss Reyes here is a fugitive, and I've been chasing her down these past five years now. She killed two good men in Arizona while she was on the run from California ten months ago—where she killed three more good men—and I'm near about fed up with her giving me the slip. I arranged with my contact at the Bureau of Land Management to get her on board for this here caper, and to make *sure* she'd be on the Harriet." Houndstooth opened his mouth to interrupt, but Carter didn't give him an opening. "I've been tracking her ever since. I was going to wait until the caper was done to pick her up, but seeing as how you've got her all trussed for me, and Travers is out of the way?" He spread his hands in a gesture of acquiescence to fate. "Seems to me the time is ripe." He gestured to Hero. "I'll even take your friend here to a doctor on my way out of town. It looks like you've done well by them, but that?" He pointed at the wound in Hero's stomach. "That's more than you can handle."

Archie and Houndstooth looked at each other. Archie spoke first. "Travers—do you know where 'e is? They were working together."

"Ah," Carter said, "last I saw, he was on a raft heading toward the dam."

"Gran, do you mind if we confer for a moment?" Archie asked seriously.

"You go right on ahead. I'll get this package all wrapped up and ready for transport," Carter responded, unhooking a pair of heavy manacles from his belt and turning to Adelia.

Houndstooth and Archie stepped into the hall. Houndstooth stared over his shoulder at Carter as the door swung shut.

"Will Adelia be . . . safe, with him?" he asked Archie, rubbing at his eyes.

"'E will not be unkind to 'er, if you are worried. Not that she deserves kindness," Archie growled. "And if she dies, and 'ero makes it to a doctor? I think it will 'ave been worth the risk, non?" Winslow cringed. "Winslow, you are exhausted. You should get some rest before we leave. If Travers went all the way to the dam, we 'ave at least an 'our before he returns. I will pack. You sleep."

"No, no," Houndstooth said, looking up at her with urgency. "I don't want to sleep, Archie. And I don't want to leave. I want to finish the job we came here to do."

Archie looked at Houndstooth as though he'd claimed to hear a hippo singing a French lullaby. "What? 'Oundstooth, you . . . you aren't in your right mind. I know you're worried about 'ero, but—we can't do it. We don't 'ave any way to set off the bombs, and even if we did, we 'ave no way to know 'ow to do it, and even if we *did* know 'ow to do it, we don't know when to detonate the charges, and—"

Houndstooth shook his head. "You're wrong, Archie. For once in your life, you're completely wrong. I've never felt so clear about what we need to do. We need to do the job. I promised Hero that they'd be a *hero*—that their name would be in children's history books for decades to come, as the mastermind behind the bombs that cleared the hippos out of the Mississippi." His eyes had taken on a wild gleam. "And we're going to do it. We're going to get Hero's name in the history books, goddamn it. Whether the job is legitimate or not. When Hero wakes up, I'm going to go and tell them about how their plan worked. And as for the bombs?"

He reached into his pocket and pulled out a slim black device: Hero's detonator.

"They gave me this before they left to set up the bombs. 'Just in case.' Just in case something happened." He laughed, a lost, wild laugh, and Archie's brow furrowed further.

"'Oundstooth," she murmured. "I 'ave to tell you something. I should 'ave told you before, but—" She took a deep breath, then rushed through her excuse. "But you 'ave spent so many years hating Calhoun, and when 'e died, it seemed like maybe you would be able to let this go. Like maybe you would be able to stop chasing revenge."

Houndstooth looked at her out of the corner of his

eye. "You sounded like Adelia for a moment there."

"If you're determined to go through with this, I'll be with you. You know that I wouldn't let you do this alone. But we might not both make it out of 'ere, so I 'ave to tell you before we set out." She looked at Houndstooth as though hoping he'd interrupt, but he simply watched her with terrible patience. She took another deep breath, steeling herself. "Cal—right before 'e died, 'e said that 'e had betrayed you for Travers. I think . . . Winslow, friend. I think Travers put 'im up to it. Travers is the reason your ranch burned down."

Houndstooth stared at Archie, then looked down at the detonator in his hands. He turned it over between his fingers, his jaw working.

"I think I knew that," he finally said. "I think Adelia—I think she *told* me." He shook his head. "Well, I suppose that makes this a little sweeter."

"I'm sorry I didn't tell you sooner," Archie said.

"No, no—I understand. Really." Archie smiled, relieved; her smile faded when Houndstooth continued, "But I do hope *you* understand: I'm going to destroy Travers. I'm going to destroy everything he's built, everything he holds dear. Everything he's poured his life and his passion and his fortune into. I'm going to burn his world to the ground, and then I'm going to salt the ashes. For what he did to my ranch, and for what happened to Hero." A shadow seemed to pass across his eyes as a broad, toothsome grin spread across his face. "Oh, yes, Archie. He will *suffer*."

Archie's face was bloodless. "'Oundstooth," she whispered. "We can't—"

But what they couldn't do, she never got to say, because the door to the suite burst open. Gran Carter emerged, covered in his own blood.

Archie screamed. Houndstooth looked at her, more startled than he had been when he saw Carter himself: he had never heard Archie scream before.

"I'm fine," Carter said, placing his bloody hands on Archie's shoulders. "I'm fine. Just a lot of little cuts, Archie, just—" He clasped her close to him for a brief moment, then pushed her away, holding her shoulders at arm's length. "She's gone. Out the window, into the water. I don't think she was unconscious after all—the moment I got close enough—" He was backing away as he told them, toward the stairs. "I'm sorry, I have to go, I have to catch her before she—"

"If she's in the water, the problem is solved, right?" Houndstooth interrupted. "The ferals—"

In the distance, the sound of Zahra and Stasia bellowing cut through the insect noises of the night.

"She's at the paddock," Archie said. "The ferals must be feeding at the middle of the lake, they are not 'ere yet.

Go, Gran, while it's safe in the water! Go!" She shoved her hands at him as though to push him away. Houndstooth noted that her eyes had filled with tears.

"Wait!" Houndstooth shouted. "Hero—you promised—"

Carter doubled back and raced past them, emerging with Hero in his arms.

"I'm sorry, Archie! I'll see you again! I swear it!" Carter shouted as he bounded down the stairs. "I'll see you again!"

They watched him leave; then, Archie wiped her eyes and looked down at herself. She was covered in Carter's blood from where he had held her.

"Well," she said, laughing. "I 'ave forgotten what I was going to say to you, 'oundstooth. About your grief and your fear and about not being in your right mind." She plucked at her wet, bloody shirt. "I suppose we should get dressed, and then we should start detonating, oui?"

Houndstooth grinned at her. "Let's blow up the Harriet."

Chapter 13

ARCHIE AND HOUNDSTOOTH made their way to the hippo paddock in silence as the stars began to wink out. When they arrived at the paddock, Ruby, Rosa, Abigail, and Betsy were already nosing at each other, competing for attention at the dock.

Archie pulled up short.

"'Oundstooth?" She said. "What—ah, what should we do about Abigail and Betsy?"

"We can't leave them," he replied. "Hero will want to see Abigail when they wake up."

"Do you think they'll follow us, like Stasia and Zahra?"

"If they do, they'll make a decent rear guard, if any ferals try to sneak up on us. I suppose there's only one way to find out." He shrugged. Archie looked at him strangely. "What?"

"Nothing," she replied. "I've just never seen you *shrug* before. It does not look right on you, 'oundstooth."

Fortunately, Abigail and Betsy did indeed trail behind Ruby and Rosa as they made their way to the Gate—following the trail of apples that Houndstooth

dropped into the water every few minutes. Archie sti-
fled a laugh when she noticed him doing it.

"Where did you get those?" she asked.

"I like to be *prepared,* Archie," he replied, his voice
dripping with condescension.

" . . . Did you steal them from my saddlebag?"

Houndstooth took his time before answering. "Hero
ate all my pears," he said in an even tone. Then he
snapped the side of Ruby's harness, and the two of them
sped ahead toward the Gate.

~

"So: we open the Gate, we hit the detonator. The ferals
flood the Gate while we watch from a safe distance. We
close the Gate. Très facile." Archie had repeated the plan
six or seven times on the way over. Every time, she pro-
claimed how easy it would be to execute.

"Très," Houndstooth replied, having heard hardly a
word of what she'd said. He watched the water as they
travelled, but it was still and silent save for the occasional
grumbles of the four hippos and their two riders.

And it *was* très facile. No ferals bothered them as
they made their way from the *Sturgess Queen* to the
Gate, though their bellows floated through the still
night air like thunder from where they were gathered

in the muddy center of the lake.

Archie and Houndstooth reached the Gate without incident. The ranger's familiar, broad-brimmed hat was silhouetted in the grey light of the early morning. Houndstooth called up to the tower.

"Hello up there! Can you open the Gate?" Houndstooth called. "Official government business."

The ranger didn't respond. Houndstooth repeated his request. When he received no response, he looked at Archie. She shrugged.

"Perhaps 'e is asleep? Surely we could go up and wake 'im."

Ruby, however, refused to approach the ranger's tower. She balked and danced, avoiding the place where the tower ladder met the water.

"What's gotten into you, Ruby-roo?" Houndstooth asked, tugging on the reins of her harness. She ducked her head below the water and blew a rude series of bubbles, turning her back to the Gate once again.

"Ruby, what are you—Ruby!" Houndstooth cried out indignantly as Ruby dipped into the water once more, soaking him to the waist. "Ruby, you damned impertinent cow, stop this behavior immediately!"

Houndstooth yanked on Ruby's harness, and she reluctantly nudged closer to the ladder. Houndstooth jumped off of her, catching himself on the ladder, then looked back at where the sleek black hippo was fidgeting in the water.

"We'll have words later, you and I," he muttered to her. She flapped her ears at him, and he was struck with a sudden sense of unease. "Archie, do you mind staying down here to keep an eye on her? Lord only knows what's gotten into her this time."

Archie saluted from her perch atop Rosa's back. Houndstooth returned the salute, and began to climb.

He reached the top of the ladder and shouted another greeting to the ranger, not wanting to startle the man with the rifle.

"Hello up here? I'm coming up, but I'm unarmed!"

He crested the top of the ladder and found himself inside the little box of a sentry tower. His eyes adjusted to the dimly lit outpost, and he realized that there were two men in the tower with him. The ranger, in his wide hat, was silent. It was the other man who spoke.

"Oh, good," came the second man's smooth, soft reply. "I was worried you'd bring weapons with you, and then I'd have to kill you myself."

With that, Travers shoved the ranger over the edge of the tower. The utter lack of resistance the man showed to being pushed told Houndstooth that he had already been dead when they'd arrived. Travers turned to face Houndstooth, a thin smile on his face and a revolver in his hand.

"Well," Houndstooth said, raising his hands slowly into the air. "I know when I'm outmatched. Are you going to kill me, Travers?"

"No, no, certainly not," Travers drawled, advancing a few steps. "The ferals will take care of that for me. They take care of most of my problems for me, you know. Cheaters, thieves, nosy inspectors. Mercenary hoppers who don't know when to go home with their tails between their legs." He took another step toward Houndstooth. "I'll have that detonator in your pocket, if you don't mind."

Houndstooth kept his hands in the air. His voice was cold as he watched Travers advance. "I don't know what you mean, Travers. Hero had the detonator."

Travers laughed—a sound like molasses dripping into the bottom of a barrel. "Oh, don't play games with me, Mr. Houndstooth. The house *always* wins." He pointed his gun to Houndstooth's bulging breast pocket. "Right there. Quickly now—before my men have to motivate you." He gestured down to the water, and Houndstooth leaned as far toward the ledge as he dared. Travers' goons held Archie at gunpoint. She looked up at Houndstooth, disgruntled.

"Four on one, eh, Travers? None too sporting of you."

"Oh, Miss Archambault could easily take on two of them—perhaps even three, I wouldn't put it past her. I play to win, Mr. Houndstooth. Now, let's not waste any more time. Give me the detonator, and I'll let you go down to her. You two can try to escape! Or at the very least, you can die together." He cocked back the hammer on the revolver. "Come now. I don't have all day."

Houndstooth held up the detonator, and before he could say a word, Travers had taken it from him.

"Thank you, Houndstooth. You know, I'd been expecting someone sly? Not you, though," Travers said, flipping the detonator in his hand. "This really does make my life *so* much easier."

"Fat lot of good it'll do you," Houndstooth laughed despite himself. "That's one detonator. You do realize who hired us, don't you? The federal government won't be deterred by one little weasel of a man with a revolver. They *will* get these hippos out of the Harriet, Travers. Your tiny kingdom will crumble."

Travers grinned, a dark joy spreading across his face. "Oh, Mr. Houndstooth. I want the hippos out of the Harriet, too! Just, not quite the same way." He began to pace. "My little kingdom will become an *empire*. Just me, my riverboats, and the ferals, from Minnesota to the Harriet."

Houndstooth watched Travers like a mouse watching a snake. "And how exactly are you going to get your riverboats over the dam, Travers?"

Travers held up the detonator. "Your little crew of hoppers helped with that, Mr. Houndstooth." Houndstooth frowned, not following Travers' logic. "Oh, yes! Yes, you see, Adelia told me all about the bombs you planted in the river. How handy! A whole passel of bombs, already rigged for my convenience." He paused in his pacing, his face shining with excitement. "Last night, while you were crying over your poor departed little lover, I was out on the water, moving the buoys they set up. All sixteen! Oh, it wasn't easy," he hastened to add, mistaking Houndstooth's dawning horror for unbelief. "But I've always been a determined man, Mr. Houndstooth. Determination is everything."

"You're ... you're going to blow the dam," Houndstooth breathed, his head swimming with implications.

"Oh, yes, Mr. Houndstooth," Travers replied fervently. "I'm going to blow the dam. I'm going to send a flood of ferals up the Mississippi, along with all their little hops. I'm going to seed the water with teeth and reap my reward." His voice descended to a harsh growl. "I'm going to *own this river*."

He raised the detonator high, and Houndstooth knew that he was going to press the button, destroying the dam. Destroying Hero's legacy. Destroying his chance at vengeance.

Houndstooth launched himself at Travers, knocking the man off his feet. They landed at the very edge of the ranger's platform. The revolver spun off, splashing into the water thirty feet below. The detonator clattered to the floor just out of reach. Houndstooth pressed his arm against Travers' throat.

"Do you remember when I said I was unarmed, Travers?" Houndstooth pulled the ivory-handled knife from his belt; Adelia had sharpened it so finely that the edge was very nearly invisible. "I lied."

Travers grinned savagely. "Do you remember when I said I wouldn't kill you, Houndstooth?" Houndstooth felt a pain in his side. "I lied, too."

Houndstooth's vision went briefly red. He slashed wildly, and when his vision had cleared, Travers' face had been slit from brow to lip. Blood flowed into his eye and mouth and ran hideously down the side of his face.

"That," he spat with grim satisfaction, "was for killing Cal before I had the chance." He slashed again, leaving another gash across Travers' face, marking him with a bold bleeding X. "And *that* was for my ranch—the ranch you couldn't burn down yourself, you fucking *coward*."

He went to step forward, to deliver a killing blow, but he found that something was tugging at his side. He reached a hand down to free himself. All the wind seemed to leave Houndstooth's lungs as his fingers found the hilt of the tiny knife that protruded from his side. *Just like Hero,* he thought.

Travers took Houndstooth's moment of distraction as an opportunity. He hit the hilt of the knife with the heel of his hand, shoving it farther into Houndstooth's side. As Houndstooth roared in pain, Travers scrambled for the detonator. Houndstooth tried to reach for him—tried to stop him—slipped in Travers' blood, and fell hard.

Travers had the detonator.

He raised it over his head, and pressed the button.

Houndstooth half expected to die right then and there. He half expected the entire Harriet to blow up. What he didn't expect, not even for a moment, was for the detonator to fail, because Hero had made the detonator, and Hero was the smartest person Houndstooth had ever met.

And he had been right. The bombs didn't fail.

A rumble like thunder sounded in the distance. Houndstooth looked out of the ranger's outpost, and saw a cloud rising through the pink morning light in the distance. He yanked the blade out of his side—it was a short one, too short to have done serious damage, but it hurt like hell. He threw the knife over the side of the tower as Travers laughed. When he looked, Travers was clutching his face, holding the flap of his lip in place with one bloody hand.

"You've done it," Houndstooth whispered. "You crazy bastard, you've done it."

"I've done it, and there's not a damn thing you can do to stop those hippos from filling the Mississippi."

Houndstooth looked over the edge of the ranger's tower and into the rippling water. His heart stopped for a moment.

"Travers, open the Gate."

Travers remained on the floor, laughing hysterically.

"Open the Gate, damn you, open it!" Houndstooth made for the large lever that would start the Gate opening, but Travers grabbed his leg.

"Don't bother," Travers gasped through his laughter. "I've disabled it. Cut the cable. It won't open. The hippos can only go North, now."

"Look outside, Travers," Houndstooth urged the bleeding, cackling man. "Look at the water."

Travers rolled to one side. He was close enough to the edge of the platform to look over. His laughter stopped abruptly.

"Do you see that?" Houndstooth asked, pointing down at the debris that was rapidly collecting against the Gate, battering Archie and the hippos. "That's the front of the wave. You blew the dam, Travers. All the water that was behind that dam is headed our way, and it's going to carry *everything* with it."

Travers grinned, pulling himself to his feet. He needed both hands to do it; when he dropped his hand from his face, his skin fell open in a ghastly gash. "Well," he said, "good thing I'm up here, isn't it? The waters won't be rising above thirty feet. Looks like all those ferals will be trapped against the Gate, hmm? And I'm sure they'll be hungry." He placed a hand firmly on Houndstooth's back. "Enjoy the flood, Houndstooth."

He pushed hard, and Houndstooth flipped over the railing, falling into the rising waters of the Harriet.

Chapter 14

ARCHIE WATCHED THE CLOUD of dust billow across the horizon as the dam blew. A wave emerged out of the spray falling detritus, a huge ripple that didn't crest but instead grew as it approached. Even at a distance, it was big enough that she could see the shadows it pushed ahead: boats, buoys, ferals.

She watched as Travers shoved Houndstooth over the edge of the ranger's outpost. She watched as he fell.

In the moment before Houndstooth hit the water, the wave hit the Gate. Archie, Rosa, Betsy, Abigail, and Ruby all rode the swell, slamming into the Gate as the wave broke against it. Betsy let out a pained roar before the water crested over her head.

Houndstooth slammed into the Gate next to Ruby. Archie suspected that this was no accident—the Cambridge Black had watched her hopper closely as he fell. A moment later, he was on Ruby's back, looking dazed and sodden but whole. Archie breathed a sigh of relief at the sight of Houndstooth, safe.

Then she realized that none of them were safe at all.

Behind her, two of Travers' goons screamed. Archie turned to see their mangled bodies, trapped between the Gate and a weather-beaten canoe. The current—fast, now, and relentless—kept the canoe pressed against them, and the water rose intermittently over their heads. They struggled in vain to free themselves.

Archie urged Rosa forward with only a moment of hesitation, but before she could reach the men, a shadow loomed overhead. She wheeled Rosa around and saw Houndstooth, already fleeing along the length of the Gate. Archie followed him, pressing Rosa forward, trying to get out of the path of the fast-approaching *Sturgess Queen*.

Travers' other riverboats were tethered, docked, anchored hard; they would have flipped over and sunk under the wave. But the *Sturgess Queen* was designed to tool around the Harriet, providing gamblers with a constantly changing view of the scenery. The huge wave had swept it to the Gate, and it nearly filled the narrow passage. Archie looked over her shoulder and could see nothing but the planks of the boat as it rushed toward her.

Rosa slammed into the sentry tower with all the force of her three thousand pounds. Archie pressed herself against the hippo's back as the boat barrelled toward her. In front of her, Houndstooth did the same, pressing one hand against the stone of the tower as if it could steady him.

And then the boat was passing them. Not missing them—the leg of Archie's breeches tore open and she felt half of her skin go with the fabric—but not striking them. Not killing them.

The boat slammed into the Gate with a deafening crash.

The current was strong, and the *Sturgess Queen* was massive—but the Gate was bigger. The Gate was stronger. It groaned under the impact of the riverboat, but it held. The water at the base of the boat flushed pink with the pulp of the two men who had been crushed against the grate. The debris that the current pushed toward it gathered against the hull of the *Sturgess Queen*: sticks and leaves and a half-rotted rowboat. As Archie watched, a tiny, squirming hop poked its head out of the water, scrabbling against the side of the boat.

Travers' two remaining goons eased around the corner of the sentry tower. They didn't seem to notice Archie and Houndstooth as they splashed in the water, arguing over who would be first up the ladder and into the ranger's tower, to safety. One of them managed to dunk the other, and clambered over him toward the ladder. The man in the water reached up an arm to grab his colleague's leg.

With a jerk and a splash, the man disappeared under the water. He came back up again, sputtering. Then he was airborne, flipped by the nose of the first adult feral to reach the Gate.

Archie and Houndstooth watched as the man flailed between the feral's jaws. The man screamed in ear-splitting agony as his blood ran down the hippo's jowls and into the water. His colleague scrambled up the ladder to safety, not looking back even as the screams died with a wet crunch.

"Archie," Houndstooth said, his voice thick. "I think this might be it."

"You may be right, 'oundstooth," Archie replied grimly. "But I am determined to live. And determination is everything, is it not?"

She swung her meteor hammer in a wide circle over her head and watched the water as the ferals surged toward them, borne on the swell of the current. The heavy metal head whipped through the air as it gained speed.

At first, the ferals didn't notice Houndstooth and Archie. They were smacking into each other, into the *Sturgess Queen*. They bellowed and bit as the water shoved them into each other. One of the bulls let out a roar that rattled Houndstooth's very bones.

The first feral to notice them was a small female with a long crack running through one of her fangs. She whipped toward them, fury in her wild eyes, and charged.

Rosa fled left, carrying Archie out of the path of danger and far from Houndstooth—but Ruby did not follow. She let out a roar that put the raging feral bulls to shame. She turned her wide mouth toward the attacker and opened it, ready to fight. Her golden tusks glinted in the sun. Houndstooth unsheathed his knives, bracing his knees in the saddle, and bared his teeth, echoing Ruby's stance.

Water fanned in front of the feral as she bore down on Ruby and Houndstooth, her own jaw yawning wide—but then a brown blur slammed into her from one side, knocking her into the water. Betsy—sweet, small, battle-scarred Betsy—bowled the feral over, sinking her fangs into its flank before it had a chance to recover from the impact.

"Betsy!" Houndstooth cried as the little brown hippo disappeared into the roil of ferals. He looked around for Archie, but she, too, seemed to have vanished in the fray. A grey-backed hippo brushed up against Ruby, and Houndstooth jumped, prepared to fight—but it was Abigail, cowardly Abigail, *Hero's* Abigail, trying desperately to hide between Ruby and the tower.

A roar drew Houndstooth's attention back to the roiling mass of ferals, who were savagely fighting each other as the water buffeted them into the Gate. Houndstooth's safe shelter against the tower was keeping him and Ruby out of the worst of the current—but it was too much to hope that they would completely escape notice, and Abigail's flight had drawn the attention of a huge, one-eyed bull.

It was that bull whose roar had shaken Houndstooth's bones—a roar that was directed at cowering Abigail. The bull began to move toward them, parting a path through the seething mass of grey that was the feral melee. Houndstooth went cold with fear. The bull was easily half again as large as Ruby. His massive head swung to and fro as he snapped at other, smaller ferals. He was coming for them, and they wouldn't stand a chance.

Houndstooth tried to steer Ruby out of the way—tried to maneuver her out of the path of certain death—but she wouldn't budge. Houndstooth cast his gaze frantically around for Archie, but he couldn't see her, and there was no *time* because the bull was free of the tangle of ferals and he was charging at Ruby with all the fury of a freight train.

Ruby did not bellow at the bull. She stared at him dead on, and Houndstooth could have sworn he felt her tremble. Time seemed to Houndstooth to have slowed to a crawl. He patted Ruby's flank with an unsteady hand. He closed his eyes for a brief moment, trying to accept that there was no way out of the path of the bull—but he realized that closing his eyes did not make it easier to face his death. He would never see Hero again, and he couldn't swallow that with his eyes closed.

His eyes flew open just in time for him to see Rosa. She galloped around from the other side of the ranger's tower, water shearing before her, a white blur with Archie standing atop her back. Archie yelled, a thundering cry that made even the feral bull hesitate for a moment in his charge. Archie, magnificent Archie—she swung her meteor hammer hard and released it, and it flew true and straight, and it hit the bull hard between the eyes with a crack like lightning. Blood stained the water. The bull stood in the water and swayed like a drunk, his eyes still locked on Ruby. He made a single, unsteady movement forward. Houndstooth threw a knife and it sunk deep into the hippo's remaining eye—a surreal echo of Adelia's strike back at the islet where Neville had died.

The beast fell.

Archie crowed as Rosa crowded beside Abigail and Ruby. "That makes ten times I 'ave saved your life, 'oundstooth! No more of this nine-and-a-half nonsense, eh?"

"Where's Betsy?" Houndstooth asked her. Archie pointed to a small brown smudge on the other side of the water—Betsy had gotten herself out of the fray. Houndstooth blew an exasperated sigh. The hippo would have to be retrieved. As he watched, the smudge made its way onto the bank across the water from the sentry tower.

"Archie," he said slowly, "I think she's got the right idea. Getting onto land."

As he spoke, a small bull with gleaming tusks just a few meters in front of them tore into its neighbor, then cast its head around, hungry for a fight.

"You are both right," Archie replied. "We 'ave to get to 'igh land."

The bull seemed to hear her voice. With incredible speed, it detached itself from the frenzy of fighting, roaring hippos and turned on them. Houndstooth felt at his pocket—the only knife he had left was his ivory-handled switchblade. Archie's hammer hung at her waist, useless in the melee. They looked to each other, exhausted, out of options—but then, in a final, miraculous rescue, four bobbing shapes slapped into the furious little bull and toppled it.

The buoys.

Archie and Houndstooth stared at the buoys as they bobbed by, knocking the feral bull under the water each time he attempted to surface. Archie turned to Houndstooth.

"I thought they all blew? I thought . . . I thought Travers moved all of them to the dam?"

Houndstooth gaped. "Oh, my God, Archie. No. He found *sixteen* of them." A smile began to spread across his face. "But Hero made *twenty*. 'Always have a backup plan.' I told them we didn't need a backup plan, but . . . they knew better. And they made twenty, and they put four of them on a separate . . . thing. Frequency. So they wouldn't go off right away." He was a little out of breath from pain and the explanation. "They made twenty. And those are the last four."

Archie let out a whoop. "Twenty! Twenty, goddamn it, 'ero, twenty!" She laughed, full-throated and gleeful. "Come on, 'oundstooth, while the ferals are still fighting each other! If you ever want to thank 'ero in person we'll 'ave to follow our Betsy and get out of this mess!"

Together, with Abigail tucked between them, Archie and Winslow struggled across the narrow, feral-infested passage. They dodged teeth and pushed past battling pairs of grey, bloodied hippos. Pressing forward, always forward, they finally scrambled up onto the land alongside the Gate.

"Inland?" Archie shouted over the rushing water and the bellowing ferals.

"No," Houndstooth yelled back, wheeling Ruby around by her harness and pointing to where Betsy was waiting for them. "Upstream!"

They rode alongside the water, watching as more and more ferals swept past, carried by the current. They rode until they weren't deafened by the ferals' fighting anymore. Archie immediately dismounted and helped Houndstooth to slide off of Ruby. He sat on the ground, his hand pressed to his still-bleeding side.

"'Oundstooth, you're so pale—how much blood 'ave you lost?" Archie said.

"Never mind, now, Archie. I'll be fine. Where's—" He gasped as a fresh wave of pain overtook him. "—where's Abigail?"

Archie looked around. Betsy stood a ways off, farther inland, panting; there were a few new cuts marring her flank, fresh battle scars to join the old ones.

"Je suis désolé, 'oundstooth, I don't know, she was right there between us, I don't know 'ow she could 'ave slipped away." She scanned the water, but it was a froth of feral hippos, and she knew there was no use—but then, there she was. Abigail, surging her way *up* the current toward them. She scrabbled up the slope toward them, slipped; Archie grabbed her harness and gave a mighty heave. Between the two of them, Abigail made it onto the bank. Ruby nosed at her, and the two hippos wandered toward Betsy, who had sprawled, exhausted, on the ground.

Archie gave Rosa a nudge. "Go on," she said. The hippo snorted at her, unmoving; Archie rubbed her bristly nose and murmured to her. "You 'ave done so well, my Rosa. Go on. Go and rest. You 'ave earned it."

Rosa lumbered off to join the other three hippos where they lay in the shade, exhausted from the battle. Archie settled herself next to Houndstooth on the muddy riverbank.

"Well," she said. "We are trapped, mon ami. We cannot get overland with the ladies over there—the Gate extends too far inland for Rosa and Abigail to cover the distance, and I think Ruby might not be in good enough shape right now for the journey anyway. We cannot take them through the ruins of the dam, not safely—and we certainly cannot take them into *that*," she said, gesturing to the roiling mass of furious ferals. "So. What do we do now? Smoke a cigar and call it quits?"

Houndstooth was still out of breath, his face very pale; but when Archie eased his shirt away from his side, she saw that he had nearly stopped bleeding. He gave a little laugh and considered her.

"Hero was too smart for me, you know. They had so many plans; so many contingencies. 'Just in case,' they kept saying; and I kept asking 'in case of what?'"

Archie watched Houndstooth, frowning. "Are you alright, friend? You seem—"

"Ah, I'm fine," he said, waving her off. "I'm telling you what we do *next*." He patted at his vest, then reached to an inside pocket. He pulled out a little leather pouch, sealed with wax; then, he handed her his ivory-handled knife.

"Miracle I managed to hang on to both of these after that fall. But then, it's a bit of a day for miracles. Be a love and open this, won't you, Archie? My hands aren't too steady."

Archie slit open the wax and tipped the contents of the pouch into Houndstooth's waiting hand.

"'Just in case,' they said. 'Just in case.'" He held up the little black detonator. "Just in case the charges don't blow, let's have a backup, they said. Just a few buoys that could start the chain, in case things go wrong. But of course the first round of bombs worked perfectly," he laughed thinly.

Archie looked from the detonator to the Gate; to the swarm of ferals that frothed against the *Sturgess Queen*, pressing the buoys right up against the riverboat. She looked up at the tower, where Travers leaned against the railing, watching the chaos below, still laughing with his hand pressed to his mangled face.

"Four buoys left undetonated, Archie," he said with a weak smile. "How many sticks of dynamite is that equivalent to?"

Archie grinned. "I 'ave no idea, 'oundstooth."

"Shall we find out?"

Archie put her hand over his. They pressed the button together, and sat back, side by side, as the four backup buoys exploded in a glorious display of fire and fury.

A few moments later, the flames from the buoys

reached the half-saddlebag of madre del Diablo that had been left unused. The *Sturgess Queen* cracked open in a thunderous explosion of fire and splinters. Archie and Houndstooth toppled over under the force of the shock-wave. The Gate blew back in a gust of shrapnel. The blast sent feral hippos flying—several of them bowled into the ranger's tower. The tower gave a mighty groan.

It creaked.

It tipped.

It *fell*.

Archie and Houndstooth watched as Travers, tiny at such a distance, clung to the railing of the sentry post for a long moment before dropping into the water. They watched as the ferals that had survived the explosion, re-covering but shaken, swarmed him.

They were too far distant to hear his screams, but they could see his body flying through the air as the furious feral hippos tossed him between each other.

"I told you," Houndstooth gasped. "I told you that he would suffer."

"That you did," Archie replied. They couldn't hear his screams over the sounds of the ferals, but it was enough for both of them to simply watch as the ferals destroyed him in the water next to the wreckage of the Harriet Gate.

"Well, 'oundstooth. I would say this caper was a rag-ing success, no?" Archie asked.

"It wasn't a *caper,*" Houndstooth mumbled just before he blacked out.

Archie patted his chest as he lay on the ground beside her. "I know," she murmured. "It was an operation."

She sat next to him as the water calmed. When he woke, she knew, he would want to go after Adelia. He would want to beat Gran Carter to her. He would want to go find Hero, and together with them, he would want to see justice served. But for now—just for a few hours—she decided to let him rest. He would need it.

The sun rose higher in the sky overhead, and the day grew hot. Houndstooth and the hippos slept; and Archie watched as the ferals, unconstrained by dam or Gate or raging current, took the Mississippi.

Epilogue

Gran Carter rode up to the dock of a little clapboard house a mile outside the Harriet Gate astride a borrowed Arnesian Brown hippo named Pauline. Hero was in front of him, tied at the waist to keep them upright.

He dismounted and hauled Hero up to the back door of the house, leaving Pauline beside the other hippos at the gated dock. Carter's nostrils flared. He smelled the air and shook his head—by some miracle, Hero was not putting out the familiar septic battlefield stench of a gut wound. There was only the clean, hot smell of blood in the air.

A miracle.

Or was it? Carter rapped hard on the door and waited for the doctor to answer, hoping he'd be at home. While he waited, Carter reflected on the facts.

Fact number one: Adelia Reyes was, without question, the deadliest, most ruthless contract killer of the day—possibly of all time.

Fact number two: Adelia Reyes had hit Hero with two knives. The first had been aimed at Hero's heart, but had struck their sternum just softly enough to lodge there.

Fact number three: The second knife had been aimed at Hero's gut, but had managed to avoid nicking their bowel, their liver, their gallbladder. Carter touched Hero's forehead lightly—it was only slightly warm. Feverish, sure, but not frightening. Infection hadn't even begun to set in yet.

It didn't add up. Either Adelia was losing her touch—impossible—or she had let Hero live on *purpose*—even more impossible.

Before he could try to resolve the matter, the door swung open. A tall, dark-haired man stood in the doorway, wiping blood from his bare hands.

"What's this?" he asked, looking at Hero's limp form. "What's happened here?"

"Stabbed. Twice. Gut and chest." Carter watched the doctor's face begin to set into a practiced bad-news expression, and hurried on. "But the woman who stabbed them missed. She missed . . . everything, doc. Please, can you help them?"

The doctor leaned inside and called for help. A young white woman, stout and muscle-bound, appeared in the doorway to carry Hero inside.

"One more thing, doctor, please—" Carter pulled a photo out of his pocket. "Have you seen this woman? She may have come through with minor wounds from a feral fight?"

The doctor smiled broadly, revealing carved-ivory teeth, straight and white and shining. He did not look at the photo. Carter sighed, and pulled a small bag out of the same pocket, handing it to the doctor. The doctor weighed it in his hand before looking at the photo.

"No, can't say as I've ever seen her. I'd remember that tattoo, I reckon."

Gran tucked the photograph away. "Worth a try. I'd best be going, but your patient will have people coming along for them shortly." He tipped his hat and sprinted back down the dock to Pauline.

The doctor watched Gran go, then eased inside, shutting the door behind him and turning the dead bolt. He rested his back against the door for a moment, his eyes closed. When he opened them, she was standing there, waiting for him. Her eyes glittered in the half dark of the room.

"You'd best tend to your patient, Doctor," Adelia Reyes said with a small smile. "It's as Agent Carter said: they'll have people coming along shortly."

Appendix 1: Timeline of Events

- **March 1857**: Congressman Albert Broussard proposes the Hippo Act, seeking $25,000 to import hippopotami into the United States in an attempt to solve the nationwide meat shortage.
- **July 1857**: The Hippo Act is signed into law by an enthusiastic President James Buchanan.
- **August 4, 1857**: President Buchanan cuts the ribbon on the United States of America's first hippo ranch in Alabama; declares the hippo ranching industry "open for business."
- **November 1857**: The Federal Marsh Expansion Project begins, employing 40,000 men to dam sections of the Mississippi, creating a series of marshes so as to meet the great demand for "lake pig." The series of marshes are named "the Harriet" after Buchanan's favorite pet cow.
- **December 1857**: The territory encompassing the Harriet and the hippo marshes are declared neutral, free territory in the Great Hippo Compromise. The Great Louisiana Hippo Rush begins. Ranchers stake their claims.

- **January 1858**: Quentin Houlihan, a hired hopper on Samuel F. Greenlay's hippo ranch just outside of Baton Rouge, falls asleep on the job. His lantern falls onto a pile of rushes. The fire is put out, but not before the hastily erected fencing that surrounds the ranch is compromised. All 97 hippos escape into the bayou. None are recovered.

- **May 1859**: During the Great Hippo Bust, ranches throughout the Harriet are plagued by feral hippo attacks and disease.

- **February 1861**: President Buchanan, nearing the end of his term, signs off on the construction and staffing of the Harriet Gate, a measure intended to trap feral hippos in the Harriet proper and to save the remaining hippo ranches in the South.

- **March 1861**: President Abraham Lincoln enters his office, declaring that he will fix Buchanan's mistakes. During his inaugural address, he promises that "the Bayou will belong to the hippos and the criminals and the cutthroats no longer!" Unfortunately, some things come up.

- **March 1865**: President Andrew Johnson declares in his inaugural address that he will fix the one problem Lincoln couldn't. "The Wild South days are over!"

- **March 1869**: The newly inaugurated President Ulysses S. Grant promises to clear the feral hippos out of the Mississippi "once and for all!"

- **March 1889**: President Grover Cleveland declares the Southern United States under martial law, calling it "an unresolvable den of thieves, mercenaries, hoppers, and scoundrels"—but promising to maintain a steady flow of subsidies to the hippo ranches that feed the rest of the country.

About the Author

SARAH GAILEY is a Bay Area native and an unabashed bibliophile. She lives and works in beautiful Oakland, California. She enjoys painting, baking, vulgar embroidery, and writing stories about murder and monsters. Her fiction has been published internationally; her most recent credits include *Mothership Zeta, Fireside Magazine, The Colored Lens,* and *The Speculative Book.* Her nonfiction has been published by *Mashable, Fantasy Literature Magazine,* and *The Boston Globe.* You can find links to her work at www.sarahgailey.com. She tweets about dogs and makes dad jokes @gaileyfrey.

TOR·COM

Science fiction. Fantasy. The universe.

And related subjects.

*

More than just a publisher's website, *Tor.com*

is a venue for **original fiction, comics,** and

discussion of the entire field of SF and fantasy,

in a   Fic   Gailey, Sarah,   site

to   Gailey   author

             River of teeth   elf.